MW00945320

Diamonds Out of Dust

Inspired by true events

Kayla Scutti

For information contact : Arbuckle Publishing House

arbucklepublishinghouse.com

Written by Kayla Scutti

Edited by Elle Albano

Published by Arbuckle Publishing House LLC

Cover stock photos by Luke Stackpoole and Unsplash photographer

ISBN: 978-1-952255-00-7

First Edition: March 2020

Foreword

By L. Albano

Most of the time we come across a story in our lives that reaches the very core of our soul.

Writing is a difficult task, despite how it seems from an outside point of view. Not only do you need to be able to write well, but you need to be able to create a world outside of our reality that sucks the reader in. A writer must give birth to a story, and be able to nurture it so it grows into a work of art. It's not good enough to just have an idea. You have to be able to present this idea for the world to read, all the while capturing their attention so they're afraid to put it down. You won't be able to eat or sleep until the story is finished. Sometimes these stories aren't just stories though. Every once in a while, we will stumble upon a tale of real-life events with real people.

In Kayla Scutti's faction YA novel,

Diamonds Out of Dust, I devotedly followed the main character, Savannah, as she stumbled through the streets of New York City in search for the truth: her truth. Savannah's character thrusted me into a world of intrigue, riddled with discomfort and sadness.

Her stories are raw and unwavering from their authenticity. I was immediately captivated by her and her tragic stories. As she re-lived each quintessential moment, I felt like I was right there with her: rooting for her, supporting her and praying for her success. I was spellbound by the story, its characters, and everything that came along with it from the beginning to end. When it was over, I found myself at peace and felt overcome with a strong sense of understanding of what was missing when I opened the book to Chapter One.

This book is the author's second release and, by far, the most moving so far. Her storytelling is unique and inviting. I anticipate that by reading this book, your outlook on life will not be the same. I know that the bravery and perseverance that this author exuded in this novel will no doubt be present in all her future books. It was truly an honor and a blessing that I was drawn to this book. It has not only changed my view of the world, but my appreciation for the written world. If you pick up this book, make sure you pick up a box of tissues with it- you won't regret it.

Philippians 4:13

To all of you who have helped me get to where I am today. You know who you are.

Thank you from the bottom of my heart.

Diamonds Out of Dust

Inspired by true events

Kayla Scutti

- *Chapter One* -

"Savannah," I hear from across the aisle. "Everything alright?"

I untuck my stiff, curled up body from the bus seat and glance over my left shoulder. My Aunt Angela's smiling face stares at me, and I manage a faint smile back at her. Her thick, curly black hair sits full on her shoulders as she makes eye contact with me. Silently, I envy her olive skin tone and ageless face. She's dressed in her work attire, and I can smell her sweet perfume from my seat - a smell that I've come to associate with her no matter where I am. The smell of home.

"I'm good. Just trying to get

comfortable," I answer.

Nodding, she smiles, but her loving eyes show concern. "There isn't much longer to go. Just hang in there."

I nod and turn back toward the window. Seizing the opportunity for quiet time, I grab a pair of tangled earbuds and pop them in my ears. Drowning out the sound of the bus and its passengers, I slide my thumb on the screen of my phone to increase the volume.

The sun starts to rise as I longingly stare out the greyhound bus window with my knees pulled up to my chin. My iPod sits balanced on my chest as I lean my head on the back of the seat. My mind wrestles with itself from the events that have occurred in my life up until this point. As unwanted tears build up in my eyes, one escapes, sliding down my cheek.

I sniffle the remaining tears away, wiping the residue from my chin. As I toss my long, sandy blonde hair over my left shoulder, adjust my glasses, and cuddle closer to my knees, I can feel my aunt's eyes burning into the back of my neck. Trying to prevent her from seeing my emotions once again, I close my eyes and dream of New York City; the destination of all destinations. My one true love.

Images of the sun brilliantly reflecting off the skyscraper windows while smaller buildings become hidden by their vast shadows, flash in my mind. I can clearly see the morning chaos taking place: commuters rushing to work, horns honking with impatience, and tourists blocking sidewalk space to stop and marvel at the best Christmas decorations in the world. Smells of burnt coffee from the local coffee shops conflicting with old trash from the night before is fresh in my senses. Although the dirty snow is a jumbled heap at the end of every block, the City is a sight to see.

New York is where changes are meant to happen, and change is what I need more than anything else. Coming from a small town outside of Phoenix and moving to an even smaller town an hour from New York City, was just the beginning of my journey. Even at nineteen, I knew that life wasn't worth living; at least not the way I had been living it. Couch surfing, living in my car, crashing at friends' houses, that was no way to start life after high school.

Opening my eyes, I glance at the people around me. A few rows ahead are a mother cradling her crying baby in her arms. I stare at the back of her head as the baby's screeching echoes through the bus. As she turns, I can almost see a hint of pink in her cheeks. Sitting next to her are shopping bags from outlets at the Woodbury Commons. I picture her living in a studio apartment on East 70th Street and York Avenue with all the latest fashion statements lined up in her closet. I see her pushing a Juicy stroller around the city with a Prada bag and Gucci sunglasses, smiling as if she's actually happy and fighting the tears from streaming down her face every night.

Behind her is what looks like a homeless man snoring. I give a soft chuckle as I imagine him on the corner of 40th Street and 8th Avenue by Port Authority, asking for money to eat. Some kind souls will give him a few dollars as they pass by on their way to work, taking pity on the poor man. Little do they know this poor man is a professor doing an experiment for his students to show how society responds to the homeless. A hidden camera is stuffed neatly in his dirty jacket pocket.

Smiling to myself, I whisper, "I do love the city."

Glancing behind my aunt, I notice a man. It takes me a second to realize he looks familiar: from his buzzed, military haircut to the way he bounces his leg impatiently. He's dressed professionally in a suit and tie and holding a briefcase close to his body. I stare in disbelief and rub my eyes.

Did I fall asleep? I ask myself.

"Dad?" I softly ask.

He glances at his watch, ignoring me, and stands as the bus comes into the station. Darkness engulfs us from the terminal. My mouth goes dry as his broad body storms pass me.

"Dad, wait!" I yell.

I push through the crowd of people in the aisle, trying to get off the bus. The baby with the vain mother is screaming in my ear as I squeeze my way through the tight group of people. There are some groans and grumbles, but my mind is focused on one thing: Getting to my father.

"Savannah!" I hear my aunt call. "Savannah, come back here!"

Guilt rises up inside me as I step off the bus. The cold weather smacks me in the face and a strong aroma of gasoline assaults my nose. I see him use a door up ahead to go inside and I dart toward it.

I'll explain this all to her after I deal with my father, I tell myself. *I need to find him!*

Stepping into the terminal, I look around.

Crap, where did he go?

Craning my neck over the crowd, I look to my right just in time to see him walking down an escalator in a hurry. People move only a sliver to let him through. A man throws his hands in the air, clearly out of patience already.

"Dad!" I call.

Sprinting toward the escalators, I try not to lose sight of his balding head. He walks down the moving stairs, through the mass of people rushing, and out of the building into the bustle of New York City streets. As I burst through the doors, I realize my efforts are lost. I stand in a sea of people moving in every direction with no sign of him.

What just happened? He was here, right? I didn't just imagine that.

"Dad!" I shout. "Dad!"

As I shout for him, I turn in circles, in a panic. People eye me cautiously, but don't stop to assist.

I've officially lost my mind.

Closing my eyes, I take a deep breath.

"Okay, Savannah, breathe," I coach myself aloud. "You may not have a good relationship with this man, but he *is* your father."

There has to be some sort of family intuition to connect us out here. Just walk!

My eyes shoot open and I force my feet to guide me in a direction, any direction. I make my way up the street toward 41st, as if forgetting that my aunt is back at the bus, dazed and confused. A ping of guilt flows through me, but I can't stop my feet from moving forward.

She'll understand once I explain, right? I ask myself. *She has to understand.*

Walking fast is a challenge for my five-foot, three-inch body. I border on running as I weave in and out of people. Every intersection is an unwanted pause, but I use the time to scan the streets around me.

On the corner of 44th and 8th, the crowd begins to walk while the light is still red. A few cars honk at their disobedience, but I join them, taking the opportunity to move faster. A cab driver hangs out of the driver window yelling in another language. He hits the driver side door with a loud BANG, making more of a distraction for people crossing.

I can smell the burgers from Smith's bar as I pass by. The scent is almost visible like in the old cartoons. Closing my eyes, I imagine floating in the air, nostrils open wide, toward a plate of food. As my imagination is toying with my hunger, I feel my body run into someone.

"Oomph."

"What the…watch where you're goin', huh?" A man says. His accent is thick and stern.

"I'm so sorry, sir. I didn't mean to…"

Shaking his head, he storms off down the street. My stomach growls in protest, but I continue on.

It's only breakfast, Savannah. Get yourself together, would you?

After reaching the corner of 45th, my shoulders sag. Dad is nowhere to be found, and my confidence is dwindling.

Maybe it really wasn't him. After all, he didn't actually address me on the bus.

My mind struggles to recall the information from just moments ago. It's already a bit foggy.

Did I want *it to be him, so I concocted his image in my brain?*

Frustration sets in as I rack my brain. With no luck, I scan the area one last time. There's an Asian woman yelling at someone on her cell phone at the opposite corner, and a group of people with scarves and thick jackets at the other, but no Dad.

With a sigh, I turn to go back to Port Authority. As I'm pushing my way back through the angry people, I attempt to recall this morning's events. Looking to my right, I spot him and totally forget about anything else but catching up to him. His broad shoulders and balding head stand out to me like a flashing light. My spirit lights up as I race down 45th toward him.

He's walking fast with his cell phone attached to his ear. I should be able to catch up to him quickly, but it's like I'm running through molasses. The faster I run, the quicker he walks. I'm confused and I feel my vision tunneling.

"Dad!" I yell out of breath. "Dad it's me, Savannah! Wait!"

He takes a left into a marble building. A smile crosses my now sweaty face, and for the first time, I feel like I can slow down. My heart is racing with my nerves rushing through me, but I ease my body to a slower pace.

It's really him. I'm not crazy. Dad is here, in my city.

"And I've got him."

- *Chapter Two* -

I blink several times from the unexpected darkness surrounding me after bursting through the heavy doors. Putting my hands on my knees, I try to catch my breath.

"I need to spend more time in the gym and less on the couch," I huff.

A tall, bald man stands with his thick arms crossed over his chest. He looms over me as I continue to inhale deeply and exhale quickly. His smooth dark arms are muscular, and his scowl is threatening.

"Sorry," I say.

"A workout before your shift, huh?" he asks raising an eyebrow.

"Um…" I stand straight and look at him with a head tilt and furrowed brows. "My shift?"

"Just go on in," he says. His body is unmoving. "Dancers usually go in through the side door in the back-left corner."

Awkwardly, I begin to walk into the…bar? As I place one foot in front of the other, I notice a velvet couch to my right. The burgundy color stands out against the dark paint that covers the lobby walls. To my left is a small, square cut out where a girl leans against the counter. She scrolls through her smartphone and chews the bubble gum in her mouth obnoxiously. As I progress through the second set of double doors, I see the stage lights from the front.

My mouth falls open at the realization that I'm not just in any bar, but a gentlemen's club. Men sit at round tables with poles in the middle of them. Some have half-naked women dancing on them, others have men getting lap dances. Quickly, I glance around but I don't see my father. My cheeks burn hot as I take in the sights around me. Looking down awkwardly, I pick up my pace to the back corner where the bouncer had instructed me to go.

What am I doing here? I ask myself. *Maybe my dad has a meeting? I'll talk to someone who isn't...busy, to see if they know anything.*

The doorknob is slippery under my sweaty palm, and the door feels heavier than it actually is. After quickly going through the door, my face flushes more at the atmosphere I step into. Beautiful women, young and old, walk about in their undergarments. Some are completely topless and strut about with confidence. Once again, I stare down at my shoes.

This is NOT where I want to be.

I'm frozen in place and can't seem to find the strength to turn around. As I study the tile floor, I see a pair of white, pedicured feet step in front of me. I wince, knowing she's going to ask me what I'm doing here.

"You're the new girl, right?" she asks.

Her voice is soothing.

As I slowly look up to meet her face, my stomach drops. She too, is only wearing black, lace underwear and a black bra. Most of her skin is exposed, which makes me feel very uncomfortable. A mirror stands on the far back wall, revealing my image.

I can clearly see my stomach pouch that I can never seem to get rid of under my tight hoodie. The jeans that are clung to my skinny legs push my stomach up into a muffin top. I cross my arms over my big chest in order to conceal some of the unflattering image standing before me. Awkwardly, I push my glasses up the bridge of my nose and run my fingers through my sandy blonde hair, keeping it parted to the left.

"I'm Mary," the slender woman says. She extends her hand out to me, and with one arm still wrapped around my midsection, I grasp her palm in mine.

"Nice to meet you," I barely get out.

Trying to avoid looking at her almost naked body, I look her in the eyes, focusing on her face. She smiles brightly at me, the little light in the room gleaming off her white teeth. Her long, bleach blonde hair is piled on her left shoulder, and swooped bangs cover most of her left eye. Her doe eyes are a bright shade of green, making them look almost fake.

"Uh—I'm Savannah."

"What a beautiful name," Mary compliments with excitement. Her energy is contagious.

"Thank you," I say. My cheeks remain cherry red. "I hope this isn't too forward, but you're very pretty."

This time, her cheeks fill with a crimson hue. She smiles and looks down at her feet. I can't imagine that no one has ever complimented her before, so her reaction of slight embarrassment shocks me.

"Today's your first day, right?" Mary asks.

"Well—not exactly…"

Mary tilts her head with furrowed brows.

"I'm actually looking for…someone."

She smiles but shows no teeth. "Aren't we all." Mary grabs my arm. "Come on. Get ready with me and we can talk more."

Her grip is gentle but firm. As she begins to drag me further into the room of women, I pull back enough to cause resistance. She chuckles but doesn't stop pulling me toward the unknown.

"I really should be going," I say.

"Nonsense! I need help getting ready, and since this is your first day, and all, you might need the help too."

I see Mary give me a once-over out of the corner of her eye, but the smile never leaves her face. After passing all kinds of women putting on make-up in bright reflective mirrors, we arrive at a tiny desk. The big round mirror is outlined with bright light bulbs, like in the movies. Mary shoves me down onto one of the stools before pulling a nearby stool closer for herself. She crosses her legs and bounces them to an unheard tune.

"So, tell me about yourself, Savannah," Mary states. She leans her elbow on her leg and holds her chin with her knuckles.

"Oh, um…well, there's not much to tell. I'm twenty-one, and I live with my aunt and uncle upstate. I go to school at—"

"Not the boring stuff," Mary interrupts. "The juicy stuff. Where were you born, who was your first kiss, that sort of thing."

I sit shocked. "Well, uh… I'm not sure I…."

"Okay, I'll tell you about me then. Sometimes sharing about one's past can be too personal. I wouldn't want to make you feel uncomfortable."

Again, I glance at her lack of clothes as she begins applying make-up to her face.

I think we are a little past feeling uncomfortable there, Mary.

She takes a purple, teardrop-shaped sponge and squeezes foundation onto the narrow part, before gently patting it under her eyes. I watch, not really sure what else to do or where else to look seeing as women continue to walk around us. With ease and routine, she covers her already perfect face with a layer of foundation.

"Well, it all started when I was twelve… actually, it started when I was born. What a mistake that was."

"No, don't say that," I pleaded with concern.

"It's true. Some days I wonder why they even bothered having me. Especially if they didn't want to be in my life."

"Your life is worth so much more than this, Mary," I say looking around.

Mary chuckles and looks at me. "You're sweet, Savannah, but it's not."

I sit silently while my stomach knots up. She gives me a small, forced smile before turning back to the mirror with her eyeshadow brush. Gently, she gathers a dark blue color on the bristles and blows the excess off the tip.

"My parents have been divorced since I was two when my mother left my father. She took me and moved across the country without him knowing, until she called and said she wanted a divorce. You'd think he would put up a fight, ya know? I mean, if I had a kid, and someone took them without my knowledge or consent, I'd be pissed!"

I nod in agreement but stay silent.

"But, no, he didn't care that she took me. Our relationship basically ended before it even began."

After finishing both her eyes with the blue, she cleaned it off and went for a bright, sparkly white. This time, she used broad strokes to cover up to her thin eyebrows.

"Naturally," she continued without hesitation, "my mom was lonely. I get it, really. It must have been hard raising a child alone and not having that companionship to counter balance it. I'm honestly not even sure she knew how it affected me; having men in and out of my life. She doesn't think that she dated a lot, and I guess in retrospect she was right, but at the time, it felt like a lot."

"That must have been really hard to deal with."

"Yeah, I mean, it makes a kid feel disposable, ya know? Plus, it made it hard to get attached to people because I always felt like they would leave me sooner or later."

I nod in understanding.

"When I was three, she found a man that was…interesting." She hesitates. "I don't remember everything about him, but I remember enough to still give me nightmares."

Cocking my head, I look at her, silently asking her to continue.

"From three to six he was my 'daddy.' I had to call him that. During that time, I was really into basketball and he was my coach. I remember I had to run around the court after practice if I was bad or didn't do a layup right. Most days I would get sick and throw up in the grass because he pushed me too hard. I was five."

My mouth drops and I place my hand lightly over it.

"Some days, if I was in trouble, he would spank me with a belt. I mean, I know that kids get disciplined, ya know? It's a thing. But, with a belt? I used to try and get away from him by crawling under the table, but he would snatch my leg and I would be in even more trouble."

Tears well up in my eyes as she tells her story of clear abuse. My mind is so busy trying to comprehend it, that it can't form words to comfort her.

"I remember this one time, I can't remember why, my closet was messy or something and he was livid. He was just an angry person. My mom wasn't home, and he actually locked me in the closet and left the apartment. Like, full on, trapped me and left me. Come to think of it, that's probably where my claustrophobia started!"

"Where was your mom during all of this?" I ask in almost a whisper. "Did she care that this was happening to you?"

Mary places the brush down slowly and stares at the counter. For a long moment she contemplates the question.

"I truly don't think she knew. I'm not sure it would have made much of a difference, because he was abusive to her too. Like, this one time, they were arguing about something; my little head couldn't understand their problems, and he punched a hole through the wall. He would hit her often. I would see bruises on her arms a lot as a kid. I think she was trapped as much as I was, but I don't think she did it on purpose. "

Nodding again, I hug my arms tight around my chest.

"Did you ever talk to her about it?"

"Well, she denied it for a long time. I get it though, she didn't want to feel vulnerable or weak. When I was nineteen, she finally admitted to it and said that she was young, which is true, and had her own demons she was dealing with. I totally understand that, ya know? Like, how can you be strong enough to protect someone else when you can barely protect yourself?"

I sigh, not fully agreeing with that aspect, but not sharing my thoughts in fear of offending her.

"After she left him, a few more men came and went, but eventually she finally settled on a man that I actually liked. I was about ten at the time, and he treated me so well. We would dance around the living room to his music from the eighties and he taught me how to throw a football. It was such a great change to the life we had lived up until that point."

A smile crosses my face.

"He even taught me about religion and was the reason I became a Christian. One night, he was reading the Bible to me before bed, and he asked me if it would be okay if he married my mother. It was all so…nice."

Tears roll down Mary's face, leaving a trail in her makeup. As I watch her pat at the wetness on her cheek, a tear escapes my own eye. She clears her throat and perks her sagging shoulders up.

"Well, it all happens for a reason, right?" she smiles.

I shake my head. "No, I don't believe that."

Mary looks at me with furrowed brows.

"There's not always a reason for our pain. Sometimes, it's just because people let us down. Sometimes, it's because of their own pain that is left unhandled. I believe that situations arise and it's how we choose to deal with it. Not always because it's meant to happen."

Mary sits and contemplates my words. The eyeliner pen in her hand shakes as she lifts it to her lid.

"So, if everything was good, how did you end up here?"

Her head swivels toward me. She meets my eyes before sadly looking down.

"They kicked me out before high school was over. I'm not exactly sure why, but her husband told me that I had to find somewhere else to go. At first, I lived with my boyfriend and his parents, but they were drug addicts. It was a loving environment, but a dangerous one too. Not to mention, he and I weren't destined to be together forever."

Leaning closer to the mirror, Mary applied the mascara. Eyes wide and mouth slightly parted, she carefully coated her lashes. I watched, mesmerized. She was fascinating to me; the kind of girl I wanted to be, but didn't have the genes to become.

"Your first love isn't always your true love. We were toxic for each other later on in our relationship. He lied… a lot, and I loved him with as much as I knew how to love at that time. With my past though, it was more the desperation of wanting to be loved. I still care about him, but differently, ya know?

Eventually, we broke up and I couch surfed. After ending up in an apartment with someone from my high school I had just met through a mutual friend, I realized, it was either this or nothing. So, I took the first job I could get to pay bills."

After finishing the final touches of her blush, she leans forward and looks at the mask staring back at her. She smiles wide, showing her perfect teeth again, but her eyes are glossy with tears. It's as if the person staring at the mirror is hollow inside.

"You know," she breaks her silence, "People have two opinions of this profession. Either you are a dirty whore who isn't worthy of anything or they think this life is so glamorous. We wear sexy clothes, high heels, and get dolled up every day. The money is *real*, and if you play it right, it only takes a few days a week to pay for all your bills. There are only a few men that cross the line..."

She turns her whole body toward me and crosses her legs once more.

"But this job...this way of living...it's soul sucking. I had dreams, ya know? I wanted to help people who had trials in their lives like mine, but I ended up here with no way to escape." Her hands sit open on her lap and she drops her head into them. "All I want is to be loved, Savannah. For my mom to ask me to come home. For my father to pick up the phone and call. All I want is to be important to someone."

My mouth drops open and my heart thumps loudly in my chest. I feel as if Mary has crawled into my brain. These same feelings and emotions have been swirling around inside of me for years.

I rush over to Mary's side and throw my arms around her. She cries in her hands as I rock her back and forth, in the hopes of comforting this perfect stranger. Tears slide down my face as I re-live the pain of my own life in my head. I had been holding back my tears for so long, but listening to Mary's story has opened the floodgates.

"I'm sorry," Mary whispers. "This is so inappropriate."

I stand and use my sleeve to dry my face. "No, it's totally okay. Sometimes we need a good cry in order to move on."

I say this mostly to myself. Mary looks up at me with mascara running down her perfect face, and smiles. Reaching around her, I grab a tissue from the desk and hand it to her. She pats at her face, but the black streaks are far passed patting.

"Here's the corset ya wanted to borrow."

The voice makes me jump. I grab at my heart as I turn to face the person who snuck up on us. Closing my eyes and taking a deep breath, I smile at her. The red headed woman doesn't smile back. Instead, she snaps her gum at me and holds out a black corset with hot pink lace.

Waiting for Mary to take the piece of clothing, I realize that my hand that had grabbed at my heart is touching bare skin. Gently, I rub my fingers on my chest trying to process the fact that I don't feel the cloth of my sweater.

"Well? Are ya gonna take it or nah?" she snaps.

I look at her with one eyebrow arched. Looking down at the seat next to me, I notice that Mary is gone: vanished into thin air. Worse, I look into the mirror and see that I am only wearing my bra and underwear. My eyes bulge out of my head as I stare at my reflection in horror. A full face of makeup stares back at me.

The woman throws the corset on the table, with annoyance. My mouth drops to the floor as I watch her walk away.

What in God's name is going on?

"Oh," the woman swirls around on the heels of her stilettos. "Ya might want to clean up ya face. Ya got a little bit of mascara right here." She points sarcastically at her cheek before chuckling and sauntering off.

- *Chapter Three* -

My head spins as I try to process what just happened. I stare at the stool that I was sitting on. Then the one that Mary had been on, and I look up at the mirror. The reflection is me, but I don't recognize myself. I have bright blonde hair, almost white, a ridiculous amount of make-up on that is running down my face from my tears and barely any clothes on.

I hold my arms tight around my midsection, elbows close to my body. A small pouch protrudes from my stomach, exposing all of my insecurities along with it. My breath becomes fast and short as I close my eyes in fear.

She was here. You were talking to her, consoling her. You're not crazy, Savannah. You're not crazy.

Opening my eyes, I see the corset sitting in a heap on the table. Quickly, I slip it on, in hopes of coving up *some* parts of me. The back is laced with hot pink ribbon that I can't reach, and the front is a plethora of hooks that take my shaking fingers much longer than I intended to do up. Tears drip from my chin. The amount of confusion, fear, and vulnerability I feel is overwhelming. I can't control my emotions like I usual do.

Sniffing, I shift from one foot to another. My feet are like ice, partly from adrenaline, but mostly from the frozen tile that I am standing on. As if dancing, I bounce back and forth on my toes. The frizzy red headed lady who lent me the corset comes up behind me again.

"Girl, get ya shoes on!" she commands.

"I…I don't have any…" I stutter. The lump in my throat grows as I hold back tears.

She lightly pushes me back to sit on the

chair that Mary had been in just moments ago. Roughly, she takes my leg, and fastens a high heel shoe to the bottom of my right foot, shoves it down, and repeats the process with my left.

"These aren't mine," I protest.

"No…" she says sarcastically. Her eyes wide. "They're mine," she pauses. "Again, just give 'em back after ya shift."

Her Brooklyn accent is thick and it makes me smile. She hides her own closed lipped grin.

"Don't get used ta this, 'kay? I'm just helpin' a sista out, is awl."

I nod and try not to smile wider. She meets my eyes, and I see that hers are struggling to gleam, similarly to Mary's. My smile fades, and the frizzy haired lady slaps her thighs before standing.

"Ya want me ta tighten that for ya?" she asks.

Holding tight to the corset to make sure it doesn't slip off, exposing more of me than I would like to share, again, I nod, but words don't escape my lips. Standing, I stumble a bit from the sudden height. She grabs my elbow to steady me. Without words, I turn around and feel her tighten the hot pink ribbon. She laces them to keep it in place.

Turning me around, she looks me up and down before flipping her large head of hair from one side to the other. She chews her lip with narrowed eyes. I feel like a monkey on display. Goosebumps spread across my arms from the sheer embarrassment and panic I feel from my crunched up toes to the tips of my blonde hair.

"I'm not feelin' the shoes with tha corset." She places a finger to her lips as she continues to study me. "Awe well, time's up, buttercup. Our shift's started and you know how Phil gets when we're late."

With that, Frizzy Hair grabs my wrist and drags me across the room. The heels on my feet slide on the tiled floor as I try to stop her. My mouth tingles as bile starts to rise from my stomach.

You can't go out there looking like this!

Savannah!

The voice inside of me shouts, but the words get caught in my throat. I close my eyes as she opens the door and pulls me through it. My heart is racing as I see the image of the reflection in my mind's eye. I feel my cheeks burning. Slowly, I open my eyes to a dark room full of tables. I'm back where I began, but this time, exposed. I cross my arms over my chest, not exactly sure how to cover my whole body at once. The stage is brightly lit to my left and there are circular tables with poles centered in their middle. Many have women dancing on them, but some are empty, waiting for the next shift of ladies to start.

I stand, frozen, not sure where to go, when a man walks up to me. His hair is slicked back and he has a freaky looking goatee around his mouth. He licks his lips and I close my eyes, fighting the tears back.

"Well, hello there," he says.

Automatically, my feet start moving. My sight is set on the heavy double doors, and nothing in my path will block me from exiting this hellhole. I manage to dodge my way around the creep in front of me with my arms still crossed. Sighing in relief, I focus on my goal. That's when another man jumps in front of me. His baby face is bare and his breath is strong from whiskey.

I cringe as tears begin to roll down my made up face. The strands of long blonde hair laying on my chest.

"How 'bout a lap dance, doll?" he slurs.

I duck as he attempts to put his arm around me and quickly speed off toward the doors. My heart races once I feel an ice cold hand around my right elbow. The man is pulling me back toward him and I scream out in panic.

"Are you gonna do your job, or what, slut?"

"Let go of me!" I yell. I uncross my arms and try to pry his tight fingers off my body.

Tears flood my eyes. My heart thumps in my chest. The sounds around me muffle. All I can see is this hungry look in the man's eyes.

They glaze over and I see him lick his lips. Sheer panic fills my body as the Unsolved Mysteries song plays in my head.

I want out. I pry. *Please, God, get me out of here. He's going to kill me, isn't he?*

Suddenly, I see a ball of red storming towards us. The frizzy haired woman from before has steam coming out of her ears as she marches toward the man. He's so fixated on me that he doesn't see it coming. She leans back, cocking her arm, and uses the force of her body to plow her fist right through the man's jaw. He lets go of me, falling straight to the ground. I stand in awe, my mouth gaping.

"This is a hands free zone, bastard!" she yells at the pile of flesh on the floor.

He lays, rubbing his jaw with his right hand. Between the shock of her force and the multiple drinks in his system, the man doesn't make any attempt to get up.

She looks at me with telling eyes.

"Thank you," I whisper.

Quickly, I walk toward the door praying I don't have any more run-ins. After bursting through the first set of double doors, I see my father. He exchanges a ticket for his coat, before draping it over his arm.

"Oh my gosh, Dad!" I say. "I thought I wasn't going to find you…"

As I speak, he turns, looks me over for a split second before wrinkling his nose, and leaves the building. His eyes never meet mine and part of me wonders if he even recognized me.

My head is spinning from this whole event, but I'm so close and I just want answers. I go to step through the door and remember I'm still in the corset and heels.

"I need a jacket!" I yell.

The coat checker raises her eyebrow at me with a head tilt. She snaps her gum and chews obnoxiously slow. Her eyes are dead locked on mine.

"I'm sorry, I don't mean to be rude, but I need a jacket so I can follow that man," I plead.

She shakes her head at me and reaches for a coat far in the back.

"He owe you money or somethin'?" she asks.

"No, nothing like that. I just…need to talk to him."

"You'll be back soon?" she asks.

I nod, knowing that I'm lying, and snatch the caramel colored trench coat from her hand.

"What? No thank you?" She asks sarcastically.

Quickly, I throw it over my shoulders and rush out of the doors back on the busy streets, ignoring her question. As I tighten the belt around my waist, I glance in both directions. My fingers fumble to loop the belt as my hands shake from nerves.

"Dad," I groan. "Where did you go now?"

- *Chapter Four* -

Instinctively, I take a left after the doors close behind me. My tiny frame walks as fast as it can in the seven-inch heels strapped to my feet. A few times, I stumble, looking like a fawn taking its first steps.

As I glance on both sides of the street, elongating my neck to see over the tops of people, I realize my father is nowhere to be found. Part of me wants to turn back and go the other way, but because of my attire, I decide that going back towards the "club" isn't the best idea.

At best, I'll just go up ahead and make a

circle around the building, though, he might totally be gone by then. I reason with myself. *Maybe that's for the best. He clearly didn't want to stop and chat.*

While I'm desperately trying to calculate my next move, a woman and her husband stare at me as they walk by. The man's eyes are wide and a slight smile crosses his lips. The woman's eyes are narrowed and her side eye drills disgust deep inside me. I pull the fabric belt tighter around my waist and gather the open part of the trench coat together by my neck. Looking down, I avoid their eyes and pray that this will all be over soon.

I can't give up...

I turn the corner tracking my father with nothing but the air, like a bloodhound. With my arms crossed over my chest, I stand at the light on 47th and 9th. My feet are hurting from these shoes, so I gently shift my weight back and forth as I wait for the white pedestrian to show. A few people cross quickly while cars honk at them for disobeying the light, but I stay put knowing I wouldn't walk fast enough to make it past the speeding cabbies.

Finally, the colors switch from red to green, and the white figure shines. As I gingerly walk across the street, I see a group of kids playing off to the side. People pass by as they shove a little girl between them. My eyes widen at this realization and my feet gravitate toward them. As I watch this helpless little girl being bullied, I'm furious that no one has stepped in. Several adults pass, just in the amount of time that I've been there, and no one looks up from their phones.

"You're a bastard!" I hear the children chanting. "Bastard child! Bastard child!"

My mouth drops as these words come out of the children's mouths. They can't be older than ten. The little girl in the middle cries as they toss her back and forth, her chubby body jiggling with every abrupt stop.

"You know what that means, retard?" A taller boy asks. "It means your daddy doesn't love you!"

A girl shoves her toward the taller boy, and he pushes her to the ground laughing. The rest of the kids join him. I pick up speed as I see the boy kick the girl while she's down. She yelps in pain and grabs her side. The grin on the boy's face is pure evil.

"Whoa!" I say. Breaking through the circle of hate I see pain in the little girls face. "What's going on here?" I ask in my best adult voice.

All the children back away with their tails between their legs, except the tall boy.

"We're just playing, ma'am," he grins a devious smile.

"Oh, really?" I say nonchalantly. "Well, do you mind if I play? I think it's your turn to be the monkey in the middle."

The boy chuckles. "Well, *ma'am,* only kids who don't have fathers are in the middle. My dad loves me, so I can't be." He squints his eyes and sarcastically says, "Maybe next time."

"My dad does love me!" the little girl yells from the ground.

She chokes on her tears, clearly hurt physically and emotionally. Still holding her side, she groans slightly.

"Oh yeah?" another boy chimes in. "Then how come he's never around?"

The young girl hangs her head.

"You're nothing but a stupid bastard child."

"That's probably why she said he was dead, because she knew that he didn't even want her to be born…" the tall boy smirks.

The group laughs loudly. Some point fingers at her.

"Who does that?" a girl says. "Maybe he's embarrassed to call *you* his daughter. I know I would be."

Again, the kids explode in laughter. I glance down at the little girl on the floor and see tears rolling down her scuffed up face. My heart drops.

"Hey!" I yell. "That is enough! How dare you say something like that?"

Again, his young freckled face looks daring at me. I get down to his level, meeting my face with his. Something inside me is taking over and I can't stop it. It's strange how seeing a helpless child being pushed down lights a flame of rage inside me that I didn't even know existed.

"I know where you live, kid. I know all about you and your parents. Look into my eyes and see if I'm lying."

I narrow them, but secretly I'm shaking.

This is totally not okay, Savannah. He's just a child!

He begins to tremble slightly.

"Leave this girl alone, or I will send someone to follow you and watch your ever move. You'll wish *you* were never born."

His eyes widen, as my heart pounds. Slowly, the group backs away before turning and running down the street. My hands shake on my knees, and I close my eyes to steady my mind.

This is how low you've stooped? Threatening a kid?

I turn to see the little girl trying to stand up.

"Oh, sweetie," I whisper extending my hand.

She grabs it and I help her up.

"It's okay. They always pick on me like that."

As she dusts off her backside, her chubby stomach jiggles. A black shirt with "Las Vegas" stamped on the front in a cheetah outline hugs her tightly and exposes her belly button. The white shorts, pulled up too high, accentuate her shape and push up a roll of fat over the top. Not wanting to make her uncomfortable, I try to avert my eyes.

She pushes her bright blonde bangs away from her wet eyes and looks up at me.

"My name is Joy," she extends her hand.

"Savannah," I say. "Wow, that's a firm grip you've got there." I chuckle.

"My mom taught me to do that. She says it's more professional to squeeze the other person's hand a little." Joy grins with pride. "It's not good to have your hand lay there like a dead fish."

I laugh. "My mom taught me the same thing." I look around. "Do you live close by? Would you like me to walk you home?"

Joy looks at me with caution. "I'm not really supposed to talk to strangers. You know, stranger danger and all that."

I glance down at myself, still in the trench coat and heels. This outfit makes me look more like a lady of the night than a helpful stranger. Again, I pull tightly on the fabric belt and ball the neck of the jacket closed.

"I'm sorry, You're right, you definitely shouldn't talk to strangers. Just be careful okay?"

"Thanks!" Joy grins walking off with a bounce in her step.

She passes me, taking off down the street in the direction I was going to continue toward. I stand awkwardly, not sure what to do exactly. So much time has passed since I've seen my dad, but I don't want to look like I'm stalking this poor girl. Instead of leaving, I put my hands into the pockets of the coat and lean against the building.

Out of the corner of my eye, I see a black figure. It seems to be growing closer.

The hair on the back of my neck stands up suddenly. For some reason, my muscles tense up. I glance over to get a better look, but nothing's there. Squinting my eyes, I stare for a moment, expecting something to pop out from the side of the building. When nothing happens, my body relaxes again.

You must be hallucinating. I excuse it away.

When Mary…vanished, I lost my glasses along with the rest of my outfit.

It's strange, though, I don't really need them now. I can see almost perfectly without them…

My mind tosses around the crazy notion of what this could mean. Knowing how bad my vision is, it just doesn't make sense. Images of Spiderman flood my mind's eye.

That happened in New York. I continue the conversation with myself. *Maybe it's not too far off from reality.* Shaking my head I conclude, I must be insane.

Closing my eyes, I try to process what has happened up to this point. The strangest part about it is the fogginess surrounding the morning.

I had been on the bus all morning, why can't I remember anything? I should have seen him get on the bus, yet I don't even remember waking up this morning.

My stomach growls. I close my eyes knowing I have no money. My frustration grows thinking about how I left my bags and aunt at the bus with no explanation or direction. Just impulsiveness and stupidity. Taking a deep breath in and slowly letting my chest fall back down, I try to figure out my next move.

"Do you have somewhere to be?" I hear.

My eyes shoot open at the tiny voice talking up at me. I smile and shake my head.

"No, ma'am." I look to my left and notice the kids further down the block. "Do you need a bodyguard?"

Joy nods. "Just don't kill me, okay?"

-Chapter Five-

Joy walks with her shoulders stiff and eyes straight ahead. I bite my lip, trying not to look down at her too much. Her tension shows me that she is uncomfortable and that, in turn, makes me very uneasy. There's a part of me that vaguely recalls being her age and having her fear of strangers, but a larger part can't sort through the fog.

We draw closer to the tiny thugs hanging out on a stoop. I can feel their daggering stares as we approach. Taking a deep, shaky breath, I look up at them and narrow my eyes. At my fiery glance, the group looks cautiously at their feet. All except the tall boy avoid my eyes. He, instead, smirks at me before walking through them and into the door. They all follow like sheep being led to the slaughter.

I see Joy take a deep breath and exhale it slowly. With her eyes closed, her tense shoulders lower.

"Thank you," she sighs. "I don't live too much further. Just a couple blocks to the right."

"No problem at all," I say.

The silence is awkward and I bite my lip again. The search for words to fill the silence race through my mind.

"So, you live with your mom?"

The attempt to break the frozen ice surrounding us flops. Joy eyes me with her peripherals and tenses up again.

"Um… yeah, she's working right now, but my grandma lives with us. She'll be waiting for me when I get home."

Trying to ignore the tension and just go with it I say, "Oh, that's nice!"

My tone is far too chipper for the conversation.

This girl probably thinks you're insane. I guess she isn't that far off, though.

"I used to love going to my grandmother's after school."

Glancing down again, I notice Joy holding her arm.

"Are you okay?"

"I just got a little hurt from those guys," she says.

Moving her fingers slightly, she reveals a small cut with dots of red. Around it, a black and blue is already forming. My heart sinks at the sight of this hurt, vulnerable little girl. Once again, I curse myself for not being properly prepared to deal with this situation.

As if I could have known this would happen. I argue with myself.

"Do you need to get a Band-Aid or something, sweetie?"

"It's okay, I'll be fine until I get home."

She smiles up at me. "It's not the first time that I've gotten made fun of or beaten up on. I'm used to the routine by now." Turning back to look straight again, she says, "I don't have many friends."

"Why not? You seem so cool!"

My awkward attempts to relate with this ten-year-old are cringeworthy. I used to be a babysitter, but that was a lifetime ago, so I'm super rusty. She looks back up at me with a slight smile and a scrunched face. Clearly I'm not fooling her either.

"You sound weird."

We chuckle. Again, I watch the tension leave her body and my heart settles a little.

"So, your dad doesn't live with you?"

"No, he lives in another state, but I talk to him on the phone sometimes. He'll send me presents for my birthday and Christmas and stuff, too. If I get good grades, he'll send a little gift. Nothing too big," she explains. "Like last year, I got a new painting set!" She smiles bright and her eyes light up.

"Oh my gosh, that's awesome!" I say,

trying to match her excitement.

Her smile fades quickly and her shoulders sag. "Yeah—this year I'm not doing well in math, though, so I probably won't get anything."

I bite my lip again, trying to hide my sadness for her. A faint taste of blood fills my mouth.

"Well, math sucks," I blurt out. "It's those times tables, right? That's the age you are I think."

"Yeah! We always get sheets that we have to complete in, like, five minutes. I never finish them. I try to, but I'm just not smart enough. I always have to use my fingers to count and that makes me slower."

"Are you kidding me? I'm super old and I still use my fingers, too. Don't let anyone tell you that you're stupid because of that! It gets the job done, doesn't it?"

Joy chuckles and shyly says, "You *are* old."

"Old as dirt," I say, wrinkling my nose with a smile.

"It's not just that though," she says. "I can't read very well either. The kids make fun of me because I stutter a lot. It's worse when I have to stand up in front of the class and read." She's choking back tears as she explains this to me. "I had to do this book report last week. The poster was pretty cool. My grandma helped me make it. The book was *The Purple People Eater* and we drew a big purple monster on the poster board."

She smiles remembering this.

"But when I got up to talk, I started stuttering a lot and I heard the kids laughing. I tried not to focus on them, but one of the boys called out, 'Fatty' and I started to cry. Then they made fun of me for that, too. They make fun of me for a lot of things."

My heart is in a million pieces inside my chest. Every time I feel like this little girl's life can't get worse, she says another thing that shatters my soul.

"It's pathetic, I know," she continues, "but sometimes I pretend to be sick and go to the nurses office, just so I can be away from the kids."

She wipes her nose with the back of her hand.

"The boys don't like me around because I'm a girl, and the girls don't like me around because I don't look like them, so I'm stuck in the middle with no one. It's easier to go to the office and lay on one of the beds. At least there I know I won't be made fun of."

What the hell are you going to say to that? I ask myself.

"I stutter sometimes, too."

We walk in silence some more. My obvious lack of comforting is weighing hard on me.

"You know what helps? Or at least what helped me: reading out loud to yourself as practice. It will make it easier when you're around people. Maybe your mom can help you when she tucks you in. Like, instead of her reading to you, you can read to her."

Joy frowns her brows at me. "My mom doesn't read to me. Did your mom read to you?"

My own eyebrows furrow at her question. "Well—no, sh…she didn't."

Ignoring my clear uneasiness, Joy continues, "She did get me Hooked on Phonics to help me though. I listen to the tapes and try to do what it says, but it really doesn't help much."

My eyes grow in size. "Tapes? Like a cassette tape?"

Again, she ignores my comment. "I heard my teacher tell my mom that I should be held back…a whole 'nother year of being around kids. Sounds great…My mom told my teacher, no, but maybe she's right. Maybe I am hopeless."

I stop at her statement. She walks a few steps and turns to look at me with tears in her eyes. Again, my heart is crushed, and I crouch down to get on her eye level. Drops fall from her lashes and I wipe their residue off her cheek. Taking a deep breath, I close my eyes.

This little girl has already decided that she is hopeless? How in God's name can you rectify that in a five minute walk?

I open my eyes and make sure to stare as hard into Joy's soul as I can.

"Joy, don't say that. Don't ever say that you're hopeless. Those kids can say whatever they want, but they don't get to have that power over your life. Your parents could even say it, but that doesn't make it true. You are smart and loving, just from the few minutes we've been together I can see that."

"They aren't really wrong, though." She wipes her nose with the back of her hand. "My dad doesn't really love me. Sometimes I think if I was smarter, or even prettier, he would want to be around me or call more. Like Rachel in my class, she is the prettiest girl in the whole school and her daddy is always taking her out to do things. Maybe my dad has nothing to be proud of…"

Her sobs grow as if she has never gotten this out before. The emotions exploding out of her are those of a grown adult. Tears well up in my eyes and I can't stop them from falling, too. Joy reaches out and wipes my tears away with her fingers. I chuckle and more fall. Joy smiles too. In the middle of a New York City street, we are half laughing, half crying, as people pass with concerning looks.

A beautiful and familiar woman stops near us and bends at the waist. Her medium hazelnut hair falls to the right as she tries to meet my eyes with hers. I look at her and my face feels numb. My lips part slightly, unable to move more than that. She is dressed in a black and grey pinstriped pantsuit with her heels, being the star of the outfit, of course. She has on heavy make-up for what I'm assuming is to cover up a birthmark on her face. The aroma of her perfume that I have spent many mornings breathing in, hits me hard.

Slowly, I stand, our matching eyes not leaving each other's gaze. Her lips are moving, but all the sounds around me are muffled. I blink hard, trying to focus my senses on reality.

"I said, are you okay? Should I call someone?" she asks dismissively.

I shake my head quicker than I meant to.

"You're sure?" she asks again dryly.

I nod.

"Okay then," she shrugs, walking away.

She smiles faintly, and lets go of her light grip on my arm before walking past me.

"Wait," I whisper.

She turns around to look at me and my heart stops again.

"Mo--"

A car honks loudly, distracting me. I look toward the street, and then back at the woman. My hands slowly go toward the fabric belt to tighten it again, but when my hands reach my waist, the belt isn't there. In a panic, I touch my hands to my stomach and look down.

Oh, God, did I lose the jacket? When could I have lost it? My mind screams.

The trench coat is gone. For a moment, I feel exposed. Without the coat and the security of the belt, my whole body is visible for everyone to gawk at. Relief washes over me when I see that I, in fact, do have real clothes on. I take a deep breath and exhale out the fear.

My breath gets caught in my throat, however, when I notice the details of the clothing wrapped around my body. Looking down, I see bright white sneakers tied to my feet. My legs are bare until the white shorts are visible. My midsection is slightly exposed before I see a black shirt with the words "Las Vegas" stamped in cheetah print across my chest.

Eyes bulging, I swirl around to where Joy stood, but she's gone. Fear washes over me again and slowly, I turn back in the direction of the beautiful woman. Lifting my wet eyes, I look up and down the street on both sides. Not only is Joy gone, but so is the only other connection I have toward reality.

-Chapter Six-

Suddenly, I'm in a panic.

What is actually *happening?* I ask myself with anger and frustration. *What in God's name is happening?*

The streets are busy with people, none of them acknowledging me in my frantic state. I walk toward the direction that Joy and I were headed before our heartfelt moment as my heart races.

Did someone take her?

I see what looks like the back of her running up steps into a nearby building. Our conversation isn't over and I need to make sure she's okay, so I break out into a sprint in order to catch up. My feet move quickly as I stomp up the steps, out of breath and helpless, as the door begins to shut. I watch as it gets closer to locking me out, but at the very last minute, I slide my foot between the door and the post.

Searing pain shoots through my foot from the force of the door crunching my toes. I yelp loudly, and pull my lower half away while holding the entrance with my shoulder.

"Well that was nothing like the movies," I hiss.

Limping inside, I let the heavy door slam shut behind me. There's only one way up and, of course, it's more stairs. I close my eyes and sigh, feeling the throbbing of my foot pulsate.

How will I even know what apartment she's in? I ask myself.

For a moment, I turn back toward the door. My hand rests slightly on the doorknob, but I hesitate.

No one has ever put her first… I reason. *Just go up there, and if you don't find her, at least you know you tried.*

"Fine!" I huff to myself aloud.

Slowly, I make my way up the stairs, knocking on any door that I see.

Floor one: three doors.

Knock.

No answer.

Knock.

No answer.

Knock.

No answer.

Floor two: three doors.

Knock.

No answer.

Knock.

Dog barks viciously, almost sending me tumbling down the stairs in fear. No answer.

Knock.

Again…no answer.

Floor three: three doors.

A couple arguing about money. No knock needed.

Knock.

Shuffling. I press my ear to the door.

Papers moving. Footsteps. Footsteps coming closer. A smile breaks on my face as I realize that someone is coming to the door.

Even if it's not hers, they may know her family.

Without warning, the door opens and I stumble forward a little from trying to listen to the sounds inside. My face grows hot from embarrassment as a young girl looks at me through the sliver of space. Her left eye is visible, but little else.

"C…can I help you?" she asks.

"Um…hi, I…uh… I'm looking for a little girl named Joy. She lives here with her mother and grandmother. I'm not sure what floor she's on, but I've tried the first few and…"

I look down and see drops of red liquid on the wooden floor inside the apartment. My stomach flips and I feel nausea building up to my throat. The color drains from my face as I stare in shock.

"Oh my gosh, are you hurt?" I whisper.

Quickly, she covers her arm. "It's

nothing, okay?"

I swallow hard, but my throat is closing and my mouth is dry.

"What do you need?" she asks again.

"I...I...um...I..."

She closes the door. I stand staring at the same spot, but the chipped green door is hindering my vision of the bloody floor. The sound of the chain rattling fills my ears, and the door opens slowly.

"I need to go sit down. Come in if you want," she says.

Her apartment is neat and organized. The small puddle of blood feels out of place. Not really knowing what to do, I stand in the doorway holding my left arm with my sweaty right hand.

"Are you coming or what?" she asks. "The draft is cold...so cold."

Stepping over the stained crimson, I go inside, but leave the door open. The teenager sits on the couch with her arm bleeding all over the fabric. My eyes widen, and I frantically look around to find something to cover her wound. Quickly, I rush into the kitchen to my left to grab a roll of paper towels sitting on the counter.

I bolt back over to the girl, rip off a chunk of paper, and lightly press it on her forearm. She sits, head leaned back, and eyes closed while I nurse her. My heart thumps loudly in my ears, and I try not to let the impulse to faint wash over me completely.

"Don't bother," she says. Her eyes still closed. "No one will notice anyway."

"I can't leave it like this. You're bleeding out."

For the first time, I look at her. She's a pretty, thin girl with tight ripped jeans and a fake blue football jersey on. Her dark brown hair is short and pulled into pigtails just below her ears. Tears flood my eyes as I try to stop the bleeding on her left arm. Her right wrist has a sweatband on it.

"It won't matter," she whispers. "He'll be home any minute and only be concerned that I'm in his spot in front of the TV."

"Who?" I ask. "Who will be home?"

"My step-father."

The bleeding lessens and I sigh in relief. On the floor is a bottle of Tylenol. With questioning eyes, I slide my hand over and pick it up. It's empty and weightless. The lid is barely pressed back on from recent use.

"Do you want me to throw this out for you?" I ask.

She shakes her head slightly, her eyes still closed.

"Do you need more?" I ask.

Again, she shakes her head. "Twenty-two should have been enough."

My eyes bulge out of my face. "You took twenty-two pills?" I ask.

My voice is hoarse.

The girl nods slowly. She's clearly slipping away into either exhaustion or…something worse.

I close my eyes, not sure what to do.

Call someone!

When I open them again, a tall, broad man bolts through the open door carrying a large pizza box and a fist full of groceries.

Without even acknowledging me or the situation, he looks at the girl, puts his head down, and motions for her to get out of the seat. He makes a thumbs up with his left hand and slowly motions it over his left shoulder. He doesn't stop walking until he gets to the kitchen.

The girl chuckles faintly. "What did I tell ya?"

"I don't get it, what just happened?"

"That's his sign to move," she says, laughing again. "Watch this." Still not moving, she says, "Oh nice, you bought pizza?"

His deep voice startles me. "Come on, Grace. You *know* this is for your brother and me. I'll let you have one slice tonight, but if you're still hungry…" He holds up a small red package, and taps his finger on it sarcastically before placing it back on the counter with the other two stacks of similar packages.

"Top Ramen?" I ask in a whisper. "That stuff is so bad for you."

The young girl chuckles again.

"I didn't find that funny," I state.

Blood slides down her arm and drips off her elbow, collecting on the couch and floor again. Suddenly, I feel very helpless. Standing to my feet, I swirl around to face the unfamiliar man putting away the dry soup.

"Don't you see that she needs help?" I ask in desperation. "Where's your phone? Call someone, quickly."

As if he doesn't even hear me, he continues his tasks in the kitchen. A few dishes sit in the sink, and he looks down at them with a slight pause.

"You haven't even done the dishes yet?" he asks.

I stand between him and the girl, sweat beading on my forehead. A young boy runs in from the open door toward the back of the apartment. He's quick, like a flash, but I see his curly, sandy blonde hair before he vanishes.

"Is it suddenly super hot in here?" I ask.

"I'm waiting…Why didn't you finish the dishes?" he demands.

I just stare at him, waiting for the girl to respond. My head feels dizzy and I breathe deeply trying to steady myself.

Don't pass out. Don't pass out. Don't pass out.

Pulling at the neck of my…Joy's shirt, I attempt to get some air.

"Hello?" His voice is booming.

A sharp pain in my left arm makes me wince. It feels as if Freddy Krueger ran his sharp, jagged nails along the length of my forearm. I close my fist and pull it in tightly to my chest. The fabric touching my skin causes it to sting more intensely. Quickly, I pull it away from my body to see that my black shirt has a dark, wet splotch on it.

My brows furrow as my heart races. I look at my throbbing arm, and see smeared blood on my pink skin from the fabric brushing it away. A gash is visibly gushing blood, which runs down the length of my arm to my elbow and drips on the floor.

I gasp.

"So, you're just going to ignore me now? That's it, you're grounded. No pizza tonight either." He booms. "And that dance you wanted to go to, it's not happening."

Desperately, I look at the couch for answers, but the girl has faded away. Nothing is left of her, except an impression of her body on the cushions. Looking back at the man, I see that he is staring right at me with his hands on his hips.

"Sir, I'm bleeding. Can't you see that? I need help!" I yell.

"Oh, now you want sympathy? Everything you do is for attention. Your mom's right: you love the attention so much that you will stop at nothing to get it."

"Wh…what?" I gasp again. "Please, I…I don't know what's going on, but it hurts. I feel…I feel so…dizzy."

I begin to sway, losing my balance, and stumble to the ground.

"Get these dishes done or I'll take the door off your room again."

"Well, that's a total invasion of privacy," I hear myself say.

It's like an out-of-body experience. Desperately, I'm trying to survive, yet I can't stop the urge to combat his ridiculous remarks with sarcastic rebuttals.

Take the door from my room? Why would anyone threaten that?

"Also," I whisper. "Why are we using food as a…a bargaining chip? Isn't that my ba…basic right as a human being?"

My words are catching in my throat, but I manage to get them out with pure anger and annoyance.

"You're basic human right?" he mocks. "Maybe if you didn't eat everything in sight, you could have that 'right,' but you're eating us out of house and home. Just growing in girth."

He stomps off, and leaves me in a heap on the floor.

You have to get the heck out of here, Savannah. This man is out of his ever loving mind, I scream to myself. *Get up, Savannah! Get UP!*

I'm breathing heavily, trying not to let my vision fade. My arm is screaming in pain and my head with it. I hear an echo of a voice in the distance, but I can't make it out. I look up at the door, still open from when the man walked through, and a figure is standing in the doorway.

Pressing my eyelids together tightly, I try to steady my mind. Slowly I open them, focusing all my energy to see the person standing before me. I see the slender form of a woman, and I know instantly that it's the girl's mother. She stands at a distance, watching me struggle.

"What are you two fighting about this time?" she demands. "I can't keep getting in the middle of you two."

"Please," I manage to get out. "Please, help me."

My sight is blurry, but I see her walking across the floor. For a moment I think she's going to come to my rescue. My heart is lifted as I hold onto the hope that this terrible feeling will soon be over. As the click of her heels draws closer, I try to keep my eyes open. But then, the sound fades further away. She walks right past me. My breathing starts to quicken with the realization that no one is going to help me.

Get up, Savannah, my mind cries.

I feel a pool of tears on the cold, wooden floor.

My God…get up.

There's no more fight in me. My eyes are so heavy and my body feels numb. I attempt to move my fingers to feel if they are still there, but instead I feel tiny little needle prickles from my arms falling asleep. My muscles are soft as I attempt to push myself up. It's hopeless. The overwhelming scent of blood fills my nostrils.

"Jesus," I whisper.

The dizziness and fatigue wins as my eyes close. My head smacks the wooden floor with a loud THUD.

-Chapter Seven-

My eyes flutter open. There is a throbbing in my head, making the brightness coming through the window hard to look at. A boy sits next to me. His face is wet from crying. Seeing him gives me the strength to sit, but just barely. Using my uninjured arm to push myself up, I look at him. His young face stares back silently.

I cradle my bleeding arm in my lap.

"Hi," is all I can muster at the moment.

"Don't leave me," he whispers.

My eyes widen and I say, "What?"

He sits silently, tears building in his

eyes.

"Are you in danger?" I ask.

He shakes his head no. "They love me, but please don't leave. I need you here."

Studying his features, I assume he's no older than seven. He has sad, round eyes, and messy sandy blonde hair. There's a small, oval spot on his temple, and I reach out to gently touch it.

"Is that a bruise?" I ask.

My heart is pounding in my throat.

As he shakes his head, a tear drips from his lashes and falls on my limp arm.

"It's my birthmark, don't you recognize it? It's like mom's."

This time, I shake my head. "I don't know who she is.".

He sighs sadly. "You always say that."

"What?" I ask. "I do?"

He nods, his curly hair bouncing slightly.

"You always say you don't recognize her, but she loves you. Don't you see that?"

I look down. "You just don't

understand," I say. "She's different with me than she is with you. You're her golden child. The one who was supposed to happen, the one she actually loves."

I find myself pouring feelings from a place I didn't know I had, to this little child. His round eyes fill with tears.

"They say you're not really my sister," he blurts out. "If you leave…I'll believe them."

Tears roll down both our faces. Pain is manifesting in us differently, but it's still evident. I want to tell him that I'll always be his sister, but part of me is confused.

Who is this boy? I ask myself.

Searing pain is still coming from my arm, and my head is throbbing and spinning. The sensation to throw up is rising in my throat, but I'm trying to push it down. Closing my eyes, I focus on breathing. The less I focus on being sick, the better.

Opening my mouth to say something, I hear a door slamming in the distance. My eyes shoot open as the boy jumps from the sound, hops to his feet, and runs out of the room toward the back of the apartment. I blink a few times, not sure what is going on, and look down at my arm. Blood is still gushing from the open, vertical cuts. I hear thundering footsteps coming my way, and my body stiffens.

"Those dishes better be done or you'll be grounded next week too!"

I'm frozen as I hear the steps grow stronger. My eyes dart to the open door, but my body isn't responding to the screaming in my head. Just as my heart is about to jump out of my chest, I see my father walk from the back door and stroll through the living room.

A shiver runs through my body as a sigh of relief escapes my lips.

"Dad," I whisper.

He keeps walking across the apartment, his speed picking up as he gets to the front door. Another door slams from the back and this time, I hear the angry steps of the man from before. Quickly, I scramble to my feet, my sneakers squeaking on the floor. His large, broad body comes into sight, and I start to slowly back toward the open front door.

He sighs heavily as he peers into the kitchen and sees the small stack of dishes. I close my eyes in fear as he storms toward me with thick strides. His big hand wraps around my cut wrist, as he begins to drag me into the kitchen. I yelp in pain as I wrestle to get away from him. After placing me directly in front of the sink, the girl's step-father lets go of my throbbing arm.

"You're not leaving until the sink is clean. You'll stand here all night if you have to!"

My breath is shaky from holding back tears and my arm is bleeding heavier from his forceful touch. As I stand, weak again from the dripping blood, a beautiful woman enters the kitchen. Her brunette hair is in a styled bob and her face is done up with make-up, clearly from a full day at work. An oversized men's t-shirt hangs low, almost completely covering the boxers under it. Her white tube socks are scrunched down to her ankles, allowing her long, bronze legs to breathe.

She strolls to the refrigerator behind me, and pulls out a weight loss meal with the letter "K" written on it in black marker. After placing it in the microwave, she rummages through the cabinets. Glancing over her shoulder, I see that all the food is marked with the same three letters, "K," "M," and "D."

I wrinkle my forehead, trying to make sense of the code, before the woman closes the cabinet door with a huff. Silently, she stands there, not looking or acknowledging either of us. The only sound filling the small space is the humming of the microwave as it counts down.

Finally, the machine beeps. The woman carefully places the hot food tray on a clean plate, grabs a utensil from the drawer and strolls back out of the kitchen, towards the blood soaked couch. Again, without acknowledging the crimson mess that her pure white socks are soaking up, she sits to eat her dinner. The man stands in front of my view of the woman with his arms crossed on his chest.

"Dishes," he says.

Suddenly, anger is building inside of me. Either from the throbbing in my wrist, or the fact that I have no idea what is going on, I'm not sure which. My heart starts pounding and my nostrils flare like a bull at a matador.

"I'm not doing the damn dishes!" I scream.

His mouth drops at my blatant defiance.

"What did you just say to me?"

Clearing my throat, I look him square in the eye and enunciate every word slowly.

"I'm… not… doing… the… damn… dishes."

Taking a dirty plate out of the sink, I throw it to the tiled ground and, as if in slow motion, I watch the plate shatter into a million pieces.

I grab the glass bowl and do the same thing.

Another plate.

A mug.

A bowl.

A cup.

One after another, I use all my force and

anger to smash them on the ground. The man's eyes are wide and his mouth is ajar, but he stands with his feet firmly planted on the ground. Before long, the sink is cleared, and we are surrounded by tiny sharp pieces of glass and porcelain.

Ceasing my opportunity, I slide past the big man, past the silent woman on the couch past the young boy playing a hand held video game on the floor, and towards the open door. For a moment, I pause in the doorway, and look over my left shoulder. The house is still, as if everyone is frozen in this moment. No one even notices that I'm leaving.

I look down at the little boy and tears fill my eyes. Guilt builds up inside me and for a brief second, I want to stay to help him. My throbbing arm pulls me back to reality, knowing I have to get away. With tears flowing down my face, I turn away from him and sob the whole way down the staircase. My heart feels like it's being ripped out with every step I take that's further away from this sweet, young boy. In my soul, I know that I can't stay for him, but in my heart, I don't want to leave.

After reaching the final landing and the door to exit the building, I look up the winding staircase one last time. Closing my eyes, I say a quick prayer for the boy, and Joy, and open the door to the streets that I pray are still New York City.

-Chapter Eight-

As the outside light bursts through the door, I stand blinded. I use my right arm to shield my eyes as I cradle my left to my chest. Adrenaline is coursing through my veins, as I glance around frantically.

Thank you, God. I'm still in New York… but I have no friggin' clue where I am.

"I need help!" I cry.

People rush past me as I run up to them.

"Please, I need help. I'm bleeding out!"

A man with a suit looks at me and raises his eyebrows in annoyance.

"Sir, please, I need medical help." I grab

his arm and show him the wounds on my left wrist. "My arm. It's been bleeding for…"

As I go to show him my gashes, I look down and all I see is my peach skin: healed, clean, and not one blemish upon it. The blue jersey hangs loosely around my body.

"Wait…What?" I gasp.

"Little too young to be having a mental break down, don't cha think?" he asks sarcastically as he keeps walking.

My body shakes while I stare down at my clear skin.

"No. No, I…I…I, was just…" I stammer.

My mind is racing for an explanation. My chest tightens and the air feels thick in my lungs as I begin to hyperventilate. I fall to the curb and cradle my arm. Tears roll down my face while I replay the day in my head, trying to make sense of it.

People walk past quickly with wide eyes as I sob into my chest. I place my right hand on my forehead in an attempt to shield my face, and shame, from them. My stomach is in knots and I feel as if I've lost my mind.

How can any of this be happening? I've officially lost it. I've officially had a nervous breakdown.

While I attempt, and fail, to calm myself down, I raise my bloodshot eyes to find a strange man staring at me from across the street. He's leaning on a lamppost and has a slight smile on his lips. His narrowed eyes send a chill down my spine which confirm the idea that he has his sights set on me.

As I look back at this man, I try to gather as much visual information about him as possible. He looks almost like he stepped out of a Tim Burton movie. His tussled black hair is thick, but the black eyeliner is thicker. A puffy, white pirate looking shirt sits under a lavender vest. Adding another layer to his insanity, he's wearing a long, gothic like trench coat with a hint of purple tones. His black pants are so tight, I can see more of him than I care to. With the tips of his fingers, he spins a large top hat around, effortlessly.

I take a deep breath and find the strength

to get up. His glare is concerning and I need to get back to my aunt. Quickly, I jump to my feet, sending a rush to my head causing dizziness. The man sprints through the busy street, nearly being taken down by a taxi whose driver is now flipping him off. As I watch in slow motion, I stumble backward in a poor attempt to regain my balance. Like a prince, he scoops me up in his arms, saving me from the cringeworthy fate of falling.

"Hi," he greets.

"Uh—" I quickly shake free from his embrace and smooth out my clothes. "Hi—uh—thanks."

This is the most awkward silence I have ever felt.

The man rocks back and forth on the balls of his feet while continuing to twirl his hat. I stand, not really sure what to do next.

"Well—okay," I say.

I walk in the opposite direction, knowing that it isn't my intended destination, but I'm trying to scramble away from this awkward mess.

"He went that way," the man says.

I glance over my shoulder.

"Who did?" I ask, brows furrowed.

"Your father."

My eyes widen. "My father?"

"Went that way," he points his thumb over his shoulder.

I swirl around with excitement. "He did?"

"Did what?" he asks.

"Huh? Went down 9th."

"Who did?" he asks tilting his head.

"My father…" I say sarcastically.

"Who's your father?"

My eyes are wide as I snap my tongue. "Well, this conversation's been completely useless."

Quickly, I walk past the man, heading down 9th. Like a lost puppy, he follows closely at my heels. The hair on the back of my neck stands up as my uncertainty of this man's intentions grow.

"I'm just messin' around. He really did go this way," he says.

I continue walking, attempting to gain some speed with my short legs.

"Your father, I mean."

"Okay, crazy. I hear you. I see you. Now go back to your padded room," I huff.

"I like your shirt," he continues. "Personally, I'm not much of a football person. I prefer Vegas…" He looks at me from the corner of his eye. "You make this look work though."

Goosebumps spread over me as I think of Joy's shirt that somehow ended up on my body. Glancing down at my new outfit, my heart races.

"Are you a gamblin' man?" he jokes knowingly.

I wipe the remaining tears away from my lashes.

"H…have you been following me?" I ask.

He walks silently with a small grin on his face.

I stop short in frustration, and the gothic creature plows right into my right shoulder.

"Ugh!" I cry out.

"Oops," he cringes sympathetically. "Sorry 'bout that."

"Leave me alone," I say.

"Okay, okay." He says with his hands up like I have a gun on him. "Listen, you know me. We've met several times. Just think…"

"Dude, I don't know you. I have no idea how you know that I'm looking for my father, but I can *promise* I don't know, or care, who you are. Please, just leave me alone."

"What if I tell you my name? Will that help?"

"No."

"It's Lamentar."

Sucking in a deep, annoyed breath, I look at him. "Lamentar? Wh—what is that? It doesn't even sound like English."

"That's because it's Spanish."

I cross my arms over my chest and slowly blink my eyes.

"You're obnoxious and annoying, do you know that?" I ask.

He slowly nods. "I've been told."

Pausing, he playfully smiles at me. "Just keep looking for your father, okay? Don't give up, he's *soooo* close."

"How do you know where he is?" I ask.

"You just have to trust me." He smiles and blinks several times. "Don't I look trustworthy?"

"Nope."

"That's…That's really hurtful." His eyes are round like a puppy's.

"How can I trust you, Lemon? I don't even know you."

He sighs obnoxiously. "It's Lamentar, and you *do* know me."

We look at each other with narrowed, unblinking eyes. After awkwardly staring at each other for some time, he blinks and rubs his eyes while laughing.

"Wow, you're good at that game."

Frustratedly, I tap my foot, close my eyes, and purse my lips. My head is pounding and my stomach growls. Using the law of attraction to make this lunatic leave me alone, I imagine he's gone and the world around me is silent. I feel a drop of liquid hit my forehead.

Oh, God, please let that be water…

Slowly opening my right eye, I feel more drops fall. Suddenly, the sky opens up and I am standing in a torrential downpour.

"Wasn't it just sunny?!" I shout at the heavy rain falling on my face.

And winter?

I hear a tapping on a nearby window. Looking down at the tan Toyota Corolla next to me, I frown my brows. A young woman is leaning over the passenger seat. She unlocks the car door and pulls the handle to open it.

"Do you need some shelter?" she asks.

Shaking my head, I back away slowly.

"I don't bite," she laughs.

Folding my arms over my chest from the freezing rain, I nod. "Hey, crazy, do you—"

Turning around to ask Lamentar if he wants to join, I see that he's already heading down the street. With his top hat placed stylishly on his head, he is not concerned in the slightest that the rain is soaking him.

At least he didn't disappear into thin air.

That's a good sign, right?

Looking to my right, I see a dark figure. It's wearing a long, black coat with a hood that covers the face. Even though the eyes aren't visible, I can sense that whoever it is, is staring at me. Narrowing my eyes, I try to see through the rain. The figure begins moving towards me. It comes slowly at first, but with time, I feel as if it's charging at me.

My eyes widen as I watch the figure running, full speed, in my direction. With drenched hair, clothes and skin, I jump into the girls car. Shaking, I quickly lock the doors. The girl looks at me with curious eyes. The windows fog up from my hyperventilating and I use the palm of my hand to wipe it away.

Peering through the blurry window, I try to see where the black figure went. No one is in front of us, or on my side, but I can't see out of the back windows.

Oh, God. Oh, God. Where did it go?

My brain is so concerned with the figure that I don't realize the fear that is floating around in the car. Slowly, I turn my head to the girl on the driver's side. Her eyes are wide.

"Are you going to kill me?" she asks nervously.

-Chapter Nine-

"It's f…f….freezing," I shiver.

The fear has settled, thankfully, but not without a lot of convincing on my part. Heat is blasting in my face, but the goosebumps still spread like a virus across my skin. I rub my arms frantically, trying to cause enough friction to warm up my body. A chill runs up my spine, causing me to shake with a quick jolt. The girl next to me leans into the back and brings up a blue and white throw blanket. Smiling brightly, she hands it out to me. My shaking hand takes the knitted blanket and I quickly cover myself with it.

"Thank you," I say. My teeth chatter.

"No problem-o," she says. "The weather can be crazy here in the city. One minute it can be sunny and clear and the next it could be…well, a downpour." She gestures toward the sky through the windshield.

I watch as the wipers splash water from side to side, not really sure what to say. The warm blanket is settling my body a little, and I'm now fully aware of the fact that I'm in a stranger's car. Images of America's Most Wanted flood my brain and my heart starts thumping.

Details. They always tell you to remember the details.

Looking around, I see some typical fast food cups, a box of generic tissues on the floor, and a purple bible on the dashboard. My heart lightens a bit seeing that this person is reading something that resonates in my life, but you can never be too safe. I glance in the back and see a duffle bag full of clothes, a pillow, some books, and a clear box of food.

Giving the girl a once-over, I see that

she is young, really young, and has dark brown hair. She's thin, but not sickly, and has captivating green eyes. The freckles on her face are slightly hidden and there is a deep white scar above her right eyebrow.

She sighs and says, "I know, it's a mess. I was about to clean, but the skies opened up, and I saw that you needed some help, so…" her voice drifts off.

"No, no. I'm just taking it all in. I didn't mean to offend," I correct. Clearing my throat, I add, "Do you…live in your car?"

She looks away from me and nods slightly. I suck in a deep breath, the air making my front teeth cold. The girl doesn't look dirty, or homeless. I sit, slightly confused, as I prematurely judge this poor girls life.

Her voice startles me.

"It's just—I've been dealt a bad hand in life, ya know? I'm not, like, a bad person or anything, but—I don't know. It's hard to explain, I guess."

Sadly, I understand what she means. "No, I get it. Sometimes, life just happens to you. The positive only comes out of the negative if you work it that way. Sometimes, the negative is so strong that it feels like there will never be a positive, but you push through that feeling anyway and pray for the best."

The girl's eyes widen and mine do too. *Where did that come from?*

This random burst of wisdom flowing out of me is surprising, yet comforting at the same time.

"I'm Hope," she says extending her hand.

I smile and slightly take my arm out of the comfort of the blanket to shake her hand. "Savannah."

"I assume you've had a bad hand dealt to you as well?" she asks sheepishly.

I shrug. "Haven't we all?"

She nods.

"Some people have it worse than others. People tend to focus so much on the bad in their lives that they forget, but in the end, we all have burdens we have to bear. We all have wounds that need to be healed."

Okay, now you're scaring me. I say to myself.

"I don't mean to imply that my life is worse—" Hope interjects nervously. "I just… I mean…"

As she struggles for the words, I shake my head. "No, no, I didn't mean to imply that you were implying."

We both laugh nervously.

"Two passive personalities don't mix very well, do they?" I chuckle.

"Not in the slightest."

"All I mean to say is that when I was going through a rough patch, I would tell myself that someone had it worse than I did. Not to minimize my pain, but to help understand that if others can make it, so can I."

Hope nods. "That's a really great way to think of it."

"May I ask…" I start. "What happened? What made you… have to…"

"Live in my car?" she interrupts.

I nod sheepishly.

Taking a deep breath, she says. "I

honestly don't know where things took such a terrible, scary turn."

Another shiver runs through my body.

"The house I grew up in was my home, but every time I said that, I was met with 'Do you pay the bills? It's my house, not yours.' The first time my step-father said that to me, I was met with such pain…like, no, I don't have money to pay bills, but I've lived here since I was seven…I mean, how do you argue with that?"

"You don't," I hear myself say. "I mean, you shouldn't have to argue with that."

She nods. "I know, right? I lived there for three years before he did, why wasn't it my home? But, in reality, it wasn't. I never felt comfortable there. When they ate dinner, I was only allowed to eat on the stairs…Unless we all ate at the dining room table, which was usually only for holidays. Eventually, I was allowed to eat in my room, but for a long time, while the family sat on the couch, I sat on the stairs…"

My eyes are wide and my lips part just

slightly.

"I could still see the TV, so I was part of that at least, but…I don't know, I must sound so stupid…"

I reach my hand out to gently touch her arm.

"You don't sound stupid at all, Hope!"

Tears run down her face and she nods.

"Yeah, I do. I complained about it a few times, but I was told that some kids had to wash the baseboards with toothbrushes, so my life wasn't that hard. I guess they were right, it wasn't *that* hard, but not feeling like you're part of the family is hurtful, ya know?"

"Sadly, I do."

She wipes her nose with a tissue.

"Some days, I just wanted to die…I know that sounds so dramatic. Again, my life wasn't as bad as other people, but for me…"

"Every situation is relative," I say. "No, you didn't have to scrub baseboards with a toothbrush, but you had the same kind of pain that manifested itself differently. Loneliness."

She nods, wiping her nose again.

"I should have seen this coming, ya know? Like, from what he used to say to me about it not being my home…I should have seen him setting the stage for me to leave. The problem is…I didn't have anywhere to go."

My heart is breaking for this girl. As her tears drip onto the crumbled up tissue, I try to hold back the pain inside of myself.

"Do you have any friends you could stay with?"

Sighing again, she says, "My boyfriend and I broke up and I've been in my car since. I have some friends, but we're only eighteen. If they aren't in college, they're still at home with their parents."

I nod.

"There's this guy, I really like…he's my ex's friend. I know he would help me out if I asked...but I'm such a mess, I don't think I could put him through this. I don't want to be the girl that he has to rescue, you know? Like, I don't want him to resent me because I have such a messed up life and have to rely on him so much."

Thinking about the person in my life that I felt the same way about brings me to tears.

"I have someone like that in my life too…" I admit.

She wrinkles her forehead. "You do?"

"Yeah," I nod. I use the blanket to wipe my tears. "He loved me, really loved me, but I was so messed up that I couldn't let myself love him back. I couldn't bring myself to drag him into my world."

"Do you regret it?" she asks.

A shaky sigh escapes me. "Sometimes…but he's happy now, ya know? He met someone who is really good to him and that makes me happy…I'm learning to be happy."

She nods slowly, processing my words. I pull the blanket up closer to my chin. The rain has stopped but there's something comforting about being in the warm car, with the blue and white blanket. I study the pattern and see a Skyhawk laid across the center. This reminds me of something, but I can't put my finger on it. Silently, I rack my brain to find the missing information.

"Does this bird mean anything or is it just a random pattern?" I ask. My eyes glued to the creature.

Hope doesn't say anything. I take my hand out and trace the white bird with my fingers.

It's on the tip of my tongue. I can almost taste the answer.

Sitting in silence makes the hair on the back of my neck stand up. I fixate on the symbol, but somewhere in the back of my mind, I'm scared to look over at the driver's seat in fear that it will be empty.

Once a Skyhawk, always a Skyhawk.

The cheer from my high school bleachers plays in my head.

"Once a Skyhawk, always a Skyhawk." Hope's voice echoes my thoughts.

It makes me jump. I had already assumed she was gone, so hearing her voice sends panic and relief through my body.

"What was that? I've heard that somewhere—" I ask, glancing over.

My mouth dries as I stare at the empty seat.

No…I just heard her say—

"Once a Skyhawk, always a Skyhawk," her voice echoes.

Quickly, I glance in the back seat and there's no one there. All her clothes are scattered and her once fresh food sits rotten on the floor. The smell assaults my nose as fly buzzes near my face. I swat at it fearfully.

"What is happening?" I cry out.

Tears fall from my eyes and run down my cheeks. I start to hyperventilate from all the confusion. My heart is, once again, pounding in my ears as I watch the messy clothes fade from view. Sobbing, I push the door open and rush out of the car. Slowly, it melts into the paved road, soon leaving nothing but a puddle of water in an empty parking space.

The flooding of tears won't stop as I stand, staring at the puddle. Nothing makes sense, but reality is slowly coming back to the forefront of my brain. Closing my eyes, I attempt to steady my body and mind. I jolt my eyes open as a hand touches my shoulder.

"Are you okay?" a man asks.

He's older and smells of smoke and coffee. His grey mustache and slicked back grey hair makes me feel like I've seen his face before. He's dressed in an ironed button-down, that's tucked neatly into a pair of slacks.

I nod slowly, not really believing it myself.

"You're holding onto that pretty tightly," he smiles.

His joking tone throws me off and I stare at him with furrowed brows. The confusion of what just happened is making this moment feel more like a dream than reality. Looking down, I see that I'm clutching the blanket with white knuckles, while the Skyhawk eyes me knowingly.

-Chapter Ten-

Letting go of Hope's blanket, I watch in slow motion as it falls to the floor. The man next to me frowns his eyebrows, but doesn't leave my side. My hands shake as I stare at the heap of cloth on the wet ground. I look back to the parking spot, and as if Hope never existed, the spot is still empty.

But the blanket... I argue with myself. *That was her blanket.*

My mind races as I try to rationalize it away.

She wasn't really there. I fell and hit my head. Has this whole day been a dream? But...

The one fact I can't deny is sitting right in front of me.

The jersey still hanging on my body. The blanket. I can physically touch these things, so they must be real.

As I fight through the understanding, the gentle, older man doesn't move. He's studying me, watching my struggle. His right hand is lightly placed on my upper back, in a comforting manner. Losing all sense of control, I fall to the ground, the blanket lightly padding my knees.

Tears pour out of my eyes. The faucet is on, and nothing is stopping them. The man crouches down with me and cradles my sobbing body. I allow this stranger to hold me because for the first time, it doesn't feel weird or inappropriate. For the first time it feels comforting and parental, not creepy or scary. Fear rises up inside because of my lack of clarity.

What if I'm crazy. Am I having a nervous breakdown?

I begin to doubt myself as a person. I

start to question my mental state and if I should even continue. It all feels too much and I'm tired. The thought of pushing forward to find my father is exhausting. The thought of walking back to the bus station where my aunt will hopefully be is exhausting. This moment is all I can think of and moving on doesn't seem possible.

After many minutes and people passing, I finally allow myself to sit up. The man gives me a gentle look, and smiles slightly.

"Feel better?" he asks.

I shake my head. "No. I can honestly say I don't."

He nods slightly and purses his lips together.

Shaking, I wipe my runny nose with the neck of my shirt. For a few moments, we sit silently. Usually, this type of interaction would be awkward, yet this time it's not. I feel better just having a normal human interaction for once.

This day. Everything about this day is confusing, but here with this stranger, it feels…okay.

"I'm sorry if I'm keeping you," I whisper.

He shakes his head. "Not at all. There's no place I'd rather be."

His smile is sweet and fatherly. A sense of familiarity rushes through me. I narrow my eyes.

"Have we met before?"

The man thinks for a moment. "I can't say that we have, but that doesn't mean we haven't."

"Huh?" I ask with a laugh.

"Well," he laughs. "I'm old so sometimes I forget a thing or two, but nothing is more important than the moment you're in. Whether we have met, or we haven't, doesn't matter. What matters is that in this moment, the moment you needed me most, I was walking by."

I smile through tears.

"It's funny, isn't it?" he asks.

"Um…What is, sir?"

"How life does that. I could have been

anywhere, yet, I'm here. You could have been on the other side of the street crying and I never would have noticed, yet, you were right here as I passed by. It's funny how life puts us right where we need to be."

Looking at the ground I mutter, "Not always."

"Hmm?"

"Well, we aren't always in the right place at the right time."

He thinks this one over for a moment.

"I suppose that's true…Have you ever seen the *Twilight Zone*?" the man asks.

I narrow my eyes. "No?"

He chuckles. "What? You've never even heard of it?"

I shake my head with a slight smile and raise my shoulders to my ears.

"Wow, I must be older than I thought."

We share a much needed laugh.

"The show is about things that happen that don't feel real."

My heart stops at his words.

How in God's name does he know that I

feel this way?

"Sometimes," he continues. "they aren't real at all. There's always a twist at the end that really makes you think about life."

He pauses, seemingly thinking about the direction he wants to take this conversation. The smell of coffee and stale smoke flood my nostrils as he breathes. There's a comforting feeling that washes over my body, for reasons I can't quite understand. I wait patiently for him to continue.

"When you think about it, life can feel like the *Twilight Zone* most days. We wake up, not really knowing what the day holds. Even if we do the same thing every day, an anvil could fall out of the sky and kill us. The smallest thing can set our path from one direction to another. There's twists and turns, but in the end, we look back with clarity that we never had and think, 'Ah, that's why that happened the way it did.'" He smiles without showing teeth. "Just like me passing by a troubled girl on the streets of New York City."

I sit puzzled.

"The key to getting that clarity, young lady—" He leans in closer to my face and whispers, "is to keep going."

Chills run down my spine, spreading goosebumps across my skin. He leans back and smiles again. His grey mustache curling upward with his lips. Wisdom exudes out of him with a sense of care.

"Keep going?" I ask.

He nods. "Keep going."

I suck in a deep, sharp breath, and stand to my feet. My legs are tingly from sitting on them for all this time and it feels like sharp needles are piercing through them with each movement, but I take a step anyway. Then another. The more I walk through the sharp pain, the easier it gets. Tears roll down my face, but I smile anyway. Through both the physical and mental pain.

Glancing over my shoulder, I grin at the man who is still kneeling on the ground. He smiles proudly at me and it warms my heart.

"Thank you," I manage to get out.

"You got this," he says back. "Just keep

going."

My sights are set ahead. I have no idea where I'm going or if I will ever find my father, but there is finally a sense of peace.

You can do this. Just keep going.

-Chapter Eleven-

Following the crowd down 8th Avenue feels like walking in a haze. The warm and fuzzy feelings from before have almost completely worn off, and I feel cold and alone again. My stomach grumbles as the distance between me and Port Authority grows further apart. Discouragement and doubt creep up inside me.

This is so stupid, Savannah.

I shake my head.

I'm going back. You're so dumb for being impulsive and ditching the one person who's had your back this whole time. For what? Someone who doesn't even care about you?

With arms folded over my chest, I turn around. The people surrounding me glare as I change direction, causing them a few seconds of delay. I sulk through the upset crowd and keep my eyes on my—Joy's shoes. In my mind's eye, I see her chubby cheeks. Chuckling sadly, I pause.

She needed me and I let her down. That little girl needed me to be strong for her, but I couldn't be.

As tears build up in my eyes, I hug myself.

Maybe there was a part of you that needed her...

While I stand, staring at the ground, thinking about the poor little girl that I wasn't able to help, a pair of dress shoes comes into my view. I blink away the tears and look up to see why this person is standing so close in front of me. My heart races and my mouth drops as I stare into the eyes of my father.

"Wh—how—Dad?" I stutter.

The tears drip from my lashes as I look up into his stone, cold face. He's not looking directly at me and, for some reason, this hurts. His gaze is on something behind me, so I rotate my neck to follow it. While I'm attempting to see what he sees, he walks around me and heads in the direction I was coming from.

My shoulders sag as I drag my feet to follow him once again. There's a heaviness on my chest that I can't escape from.

"Dad," I say, weakly. The tears of frustration and tiredness take over.

I stop walking and shake my head.

This is nuts. He was right in front of me!

As I go to turn away from his direction, I see him dart left into a building. Closing my eyes, I sigh heavily.

Gosh! I yell at myself. *Fine! One more attempt to talk to him, and then I'm out of here!*

Most of my frustration is from the lack of control I have, rather than the fact that my father keeps ignoring me. The broken promises that I keep making to myself to move on from this insanity is weighing heavily on me.

The walk is short, making the blood boil inside of me. There's no reason he couldn't have stopped to talk to me for a brief second. He could have at least told me what is going on. My head rolls back a little from exhaustion and confusion. The sign on the door reads *Fancy Nail Beauty Salon.* I rub my eyes and look again.

What does Dad need in a beauty salon?

His broad, military image flashes before me and I know that unless he has to be in here for someone, there is no way he would be caught dead in a place like this. I take a step back and glance to the windows on the left and then the right, just to be sure. The rest of the block, at least what I can see of it, is leasing. No other places are open.

Sucking in a deep breath, I open the door. A bell goes off signaling that I've entered, and the smell of fresh nail polish and chemicals assaults my nose immediately. Standing at the front counter is a young Asian lady. She's petite with a pixie haircut and bright eyes. Her skin is smooth and young, but her face holds a great deal of wisdom.

"Hi!" she says enthusiastically. "What can we do for you?"

"Oh," her energy throws me off. "No, I'm just looking for someone. A man, actually. He just came in here."

"Honey, aren't we all?" I hear.

Looking past the young lady, I see a woman sitting at the pedicure tub. She looks to be in her early twenties with long, flowing brown hair. It goes past her shoulders and rests comfortably on her chest. As I walk closer, I notice the mask of makeup that is done perfectly, but way too heavily. She's thin, very thin, and has an airbrushed tan.

"Sadly, the only men in here are taken or…unavailable, if you know what I mean."

She chuckles at herself and gestures for me to sit in the massage chair next to hers.

"No, thank you. I really need to find my father. I followed him in here, but I…this has to be the wrong place. He'd never be caught dead in here."

"What's your name, sweets?" she grins.

"Uh—Savannah…"

"The name's Vanity."

"Isn't that a personality trait?" I chuckle.

"Um—Rude, but yes," she laughs. "I guess my parents knew I'd be a vane P.O.—"

An older Asian lady comes in from the back room with a stern face.

"Sit!" she commands me.

Her interruption was abrupt and scary, so I did as she said. While the lady fills Vanity's footbath, I extend my hand across my chest.

"It's nice to meet you," I say.

Vanity wiggles her fingers upward with a cocky smile. "Nails, darling. They're still drying."

"Ah," I say.

For a moment, we sit in silence. I look down at my sneakered feet and hold my arms tightly around my midsection. Out of the corner of my eye, I grab a glance at Vanity's attire, and I'm blown away. Her earrings sparkle, catching the light just right. The necklace around her thin neck shows off her collar bone and adds a bit of color to her otherwise black wardrobe. Her loose black, cotton sweater looks cozy and the black leggings are rolled up enough for her toes to be done properly.

I can feel my jersey riding up, exposing some of my pudge. Quickly, I pull it down, but I can see Vanity looking at me slightly. My heart drops when I see the disgust on her face from my not so thin appearance. I feel tears well up in my eyes, but I desperately push them away.

"You know," Vanity says, her voice startles me, "you could be so pretty if you took the time to be."

"Thanks, I guess." My spirit is deflating.

"Don't mention it," she says.

Her smile shows off a perfect, bright row of teeth, obviously missing my tone. She looks me over and leans closer.

"There's a way to get rid of the weight and keep it off."

I huff in frustration.

Now she's just being insulting.

"There is?" I grumble. "Let me guess, diet and exercise?"

"Oh no, honey. That's work and this is so much more simple than that—Just don't eat."

I narrow my eyes at her.

"Or…eat and then get rid of it. All those fad diets don't do jack. If you're like me, you'll end up breaking them anyway. I've learned it's easier to stay away from food all together, or at least digesting it, instead of trying desperately to lose the lbs around it."

"Get rid of?" I ask.

"Yeah," she shrugs. "Like, purging."

My mouth drops.

"See these scars?"

She leans over and shows me small bumps on her left pointer and index finger. They're clearly from years of this practice.

"That's from my front teeth."

I sit in shock at her bluntness.

"What happens when you get hungry?" she asks herself.

She slides up her sweater sleeve to reveal a plethora of welts on her forearm. Tightly wrapped around her wrist is a blue rubber band. She grabs at in, pulls it back, and lets it go. I wince at the sound of it smacking her skin that is already bright red.

"These aren't all from trying not to eat, but most are. When I'm really hungry, and I can't find the will power to fight it…" She pulls the rubber band back again and demonstrates. "Voila! No more urges."

I reach out and gently touch her welts. My mouth hangs open as my brain slowly catches up to the insanity that is being told to me.

"Does…it hurt?" I ask.

Vanity shrugs. "It does a bit now, but in the moment, I get this rush of adrenaline and I feel in control again. It's truly the best medicine."

She looks up at my distressed face. Her tone softens as she says, "Nothing is worse than hating yourself, Savannah. That feeling of dodging every mirror because you know looking too hard will break it into pieces. Hating who you have become and the choices you've made...*nothing* is worse than that."

Her throat catches from holding back tears. My own eyes well up again, but this time, I can't stop them.

Gosh, all you've done today is cry! You're usually so much better at hiding it. What's wrong with you?

"I get it," I manage to choke out. "Loving yourself is one of the hardest things to do. Especially when you feel like no one around you loves you."

My mind turns toward the people I have been chasing, including myself.

"If your own parents can't love you...how do you, or anyone else for that matter, love you?"

The striking reality of this statement hits me hard, leaving a sensation in my stomach that is gut-wrenching. My arms collect the tears dripping from my face and I have this unnatural urge to scream.

"When I was a kid," she continues. "My

father would buy me clothes that didn't fit. I was 'whoa' chubby back in the day. Like, my family would give me the left-overs on their plates as to not throw it away, chubby. I remember we would go to water parks, and he would ask why I didn't look like girls my age."

I wince at her words.

"My sisters were all slender and beautiful. Yes, they were younger, but I was still compared to them. 'So-and-so doesn't eat that much. So-and-so wouldn't have a snack this soon. Are you sure you want to eat that because so-and-so wouldn't.' It was terribly depressing to say the least…"

"My gosh," I whisper.

She sighs. "Yeah…and then when I was a teenager, and I took matters into my own hands, he questioned why I did that…like, dude, where have you been?"

"Did you talk to him about it?" I ask.

Vanity laughs obnoxiously. "Talk to my father? That's a good one, girl!"

She pretends to wipe away tears from laughing so hard, or maybe they are real and she's just down-playing it.

"We went on a little vacation one summer I was visiting him and my eating habits were all over the place. I guess my mom had told him about my…purging, so he was on high alert. His only true concern was that my sisters would be around when I was doing it and get 'bad ideas.' Kind of pathetic if you ask me."

I wrinkle my forehead. "So, he wasn't concerned about you?"

Vanity shrugs. "Maybe he was on some level, but he didn't show it. I swear, that man was so hard to read. He was either a raging lunatic, screaming because we woke him up, or a neutral, subtle jerk, saying things about my weight or intelligence."

"Your intelligence too?"

"Ohhhh, yeah," Vanity says, "He used to make fun of me because I didn't know how to cook rice…like what? He would say it's because I'm a blonde or that I didn't have a decent IQ. When I couldn't spell, he would tell me it's because I'm not properly educated. He even told me once that he expected stupidity to come out of my mouth when I spoke…thanks a lot *Dad.*"

Spit flies out of her mouth as she sarcastically yells at her father that's not really there.

"I'm so sorry…" I look at the floor in front of me. "How do you ever get over something like that?"

There's a slight fire of rage building inside me that I can't explain. As I sit thinking of my own problematic relationship with my father, I bite the inside of my lip. An uneasy feeling washes over me.

Vanity is silent, so I wipe my eyes and glance over to her chair. The water is filled in the footbath, but my shoulders sag at the sight of the empty seat. I close my eyes trying to steady my emotions.

How did I know this was going to happen?

Slowly, I slide out of the seat and start to walk toward the front door. My body is tense from frustration and my mind is foggy from the questions floating around it. As I walk, zombie-like, to the exit, someone rushes past me, sending me to the ground. I hit the floor with a thud, landing on my knees and palms.

"Hey!" I yell. "What the h…"

Glancing up in anger, I see my father storming out of the salon. I roll my eyes and pick myself back up again.

"Don't worry, I got it," I grumble, dusting myself off.

As I continue to walk away from the chairs, the young lady stands between me and the doors.

"Uh, you're going to pay for that, right?"

Her snarky tone throws me off and I immediately get defensive.

"Um—what? I didn't get anything done. Last time I checked, you didn't charge to sit in a massage chair and have a conversation."

She chuckles and folds her arms across her chest. "Listen, lady, this is the City, I've heard it all, okay?" She extends her hand toward me. "Now, that'll be sixty-one, eighty."

I storm past her and turn to open the door with my back.

With a huff and a shrug, I say, "I have no idea what you're talking about."

"Your nails didn't grow in that way!" she yells.

"What?"

Looking down at my shaky hands, I see long acrylic nails with French tips. The image of Vanity blowing on her nails flashes through my mind. Cotton sweater sleeves are pulled up to my wrists and black leggings are engulfed in her light brown, knee high boots that had been sitting next to the footbath.

"How…" My voice trails off as I take a deep, weary breath. "Look, I don't know what's going on here, but I don't have money to pay for this. I'm so sorry."

Continuing to back away slowly, I feel the door on my back. I push it open with my butt, and look at the young lady apologetically.

"Sorry…"

"You can't just *leave*!" she demands, stomping her foot and putting her hands on her hips.

Quickly, I push the door open and the bell rings loudly. As I try to leave, I run right into someone, sending him flying backwards and hitting the ground hard. I wince at my clumsiness.

"Oh my gosh, I'm so sorry, sir."

I extend my hand to help him up.

"It's okay," he replies. "Thank you."

Instead of grabbing my hand, he grabs my forearm to help pull himself up. I yelp in pain and let go of him. I see stars from his sudden grasp, as pain shoots up my arm.

"Gosh, I'm so sorry," he aids me. "I didn't mean to hurt you."

Lifting my sweater sleeve, I silently pray that the wounds from before didn't reappear. The amount of blood I saw was scary, and I don't think my mental stability will last if I have to deal with that again.

Up and down my arms aren't gashes or cuts, but welts and bruises. A small blue rubber band is resting tightly on my wrist. My arm is red with raised skin and I hiss from the stinging pain.

"Whoa…" the man says backing away. He looks at me with raised eyebrows and caution.

"You no leave!" I hear behind me. "No money, no service!"

The older Asian woman storms out of the salon door.

"I'm so sorry, ma'am," I say.

Turning, I start running away from her.

"Wait!" she yells.

I'm already at the light and walking to the next street, praying she isn't following. Looking down, I see the high boots and a shiver runs up my spine.

-Chapter Twelve-

As I make my way up some street, I see a familiar face leaning on the building ahead with his legs crossed. He's smirking at me and twirling his large top hat with his fingers.

"Great…" I mumble. "I have a stalker."

I roll my eyes. Trying to avoid contact, I keep my speed up as to hopefully breeze right by him.

"Hello there, friend," he greets.

I walk past him, but he hops into place and joins my fast pace.

"I see you've changed." He gives me a

once-over. "I have to admit, I like this look a lot more. It feels more…" he pauses. "You." He chuckles to himself.

Someone bumps into my shoulder as I stop short to glare at him. "I don't get the joke."

"Oh lighten up, Babs."

"Who's Babs?" I snap.

He laughs. "Ooo, someone's a little feistier than usual."

He stops with me, his tall frame looming over my short body. I cross my arms as he hovers the top hat above my head. He makes sassy, playful faces as he pretends to use me as a model without actually placing the vintage hat on my head. I groan in frustration and swat at it.

"Ugh!"

"Whoa, easy killer. No need to get your panties in a twist," he smiles.

I squeeze the sides of my forehead with my left hand and sigh.

"Do you know what's going on?" I ask defeated.

He continues to play with the top hat. "You're not up on your current events?"

"For the love of God… what was your name again? Lemon turd?" I ask obnoxiously.

After laughing at my own joke, I sigh.

"Um…I take offense to that. First of all, it's Lamentar, not 'Lemon Turd.' Rude. Second, that's my brother."

"Oh, God," I groan. "There's two of you?"

"Well, no, there's only one of me," he laughs.

I stare at him with narrowed eyes.

"Oh, come on, Savannah. It's me, Derrota. You don't recognize me?"

Frowning my eyebrows and looking up at him, frustration boils in my body. He steps one foot back with a smile and poses as if he's a cardboard cutout. At a quick glance, I can't tell the difference, but when I study him more, I see he has a black fluffy shirt under his dark, navy coat. His chin is also a bit more defined than Lamentar's and he looks more fit.

"Clearly you two are identical and have

the same…poor taste in fashion."

"Again. Rude." He snaps back to his normal stance. Derrota places his right hand on his chest, lifts his right shoulder, and turns his chin toward it as he states this. Lightly, he flutters his eyes. "We are eccentric, and proud of it."

"I guess…" I say making a face. "I mean, you look like a pirate from the eighteen hundreds."

"Oh my gosh, do I really?" he asks in excitement. "I mean, I was going for more like, 'Voodoo Master' or perhaps, 'Vampire with an enormous mansion,' but I'll take pirate! Have you seen Captain Hook?" he asks raising his eyebrows. "Total ladies' man!"

This is literally a waste of time.

"Whatever." I shake my head and press my palms to my face. Pulling them away and extending my fingers in frustration I say, "I don't care who you are. Can you help me or not?"

"What you're looking for, I can't help you with, my dear," he says, brushing the dust off his top hat.

"So, you can't help me find my father? Great…" I groan again. "What a shock. You're utterly useless."

I huff and turn away from Derrota. For a moment, he's silent. I turn my neck back in his direction, half-expecting him to be gone, but he's still staring at me, a slight smile on his lips.

The one time I'm hoping someone will disappear.

"Is that really what you're looking for?" he asks.

I squint at him. "Huh?"

"You said you wanted help finding your father. Is that really what you're looking for?"

His question throws me off.

Um…obviously that's what I'm looking for.

"I spent my whole day chasing him through the city, so I'd say that's a yes."

Derrota tilts his head and narrows his eyes.

"But…like, really?"

Groaning again I say, "Are you literally trying to make me lose my mind? If so, bravo, you're doing an amazing job!"

Sarcastically, I clap my hands in slow motion.

Pursing his lips together, he nods slowly. He turns on his heels and begins walking. Stupidly, I follow.

"What?" I ask.

"Nothing."

"You have something to say, so just say it."

He shakes his head. "I got nothing to say."

"Yes you do! Spit it out, Derrota."

Screeching to a halt, he looks me square in the eyes. "You know, you really need to learn how to talk to people."

"Well, you're holding out on me! Not to mention stalking…if you'd tell me what you know then I wouldn't have to be so blunt."

"Excuse, after excuse, after excuse. You're anger, frustration, pain, or hurt doesn't give you the right to treat people how you want or act a certain way."

I'm taken aback by his bluntness.

"Did you miss the part where you were stalking me…just askin'."

He sighs. "Maybe, Nancy Drew, I was trying to help you. Trust me, you're not that interesting to be stalked."

"Now who's throwing digs?" I ask.

"If you can't stand the heat, get your rude butt out of the kitchen."

Derrota's frustration is showing, and for some reason a ping of guilt builds up inside of me.

"Please," I soften my tone. "Please, just help me. I'm tired and, yes, angry. I'm confused and, yes, hurt. I just need to know what's going on and why it's happening to me."

"Did you ever stop to think that this life isn't happening *to* you?" Derrota asks. "You're not just some innocent victim all the time."

"Huh?" I ask. "I never said I was…"

"Well, you're sure acting like it." Derrota huffs and taps his foot with his arms crossed, clearly in pain. "Fine. Just go up ahead and cross at the light. There's a club called Frantics. You'll find some answers in there. That's all I know."

He shrugs me off, his face long. More guilt rises in me and my stomach twists.

"Listen, I'm sorry, okay? You're right, I shouldn't treat anyone poorly just because I'm having a day from Hell. I'm tired and flustered. Your attitude doesn't help, let's be honest, but that doesn't excuse me talking to you this way."

Lightly, I touch his arm. He rolls his eyes and smiles slightly.

"We're good, we're good. Let's not have a moment now, okay?"

I chuckle.

"The only thing I want to add," Derrota continues. "Is this: I know who I am. I'm comfortable with that and nothing anyone says or does will change that. Can you say that about yourself?"

I frown at him. "What do you mean?"

"You're running around New York City,

still confused and crying. You have been gone all day, and you still have no idea who you are or why you're here."

Crossing my arms in defense, I lick my lips before chewing on my bottom one. Looking to my right, I study the sidewalk and process the words Derrota just presented me with.

I know who I am! Who is he to tell me…

"I'm not trying to figure out who I am, Derrota. I'm just trying to find my f…"

"I know, I know. 'You're just trying to find your father…' Listen closely, Savannah. *He* is not the root of all your problems. *He* isn't what's keeping you here. Take that and marinate it in that beautiful little mind of yours."

After taking a moment, I look back gently, and see he's already walking off with the crowd. A new weight has been placed on my chest by his clear observation. I push back the tears before heading in the direction he has told me to go. Repeating the name of the club in my head doesn't seem to distract my thoughts but I do it anyway.

I know who I am…I'm a fighter. I'm surviving.

Then my thoughts change direction down a more realistic path.

Who am I kidding? I'm really just a burden to my family and all those around me…I'm an orphan…The world would be better off without me…

-Chapter Thirteen-

The glowing sign looms over me.
Rap and R&B music blares from inside, only
intensifying as people filter in and out. The
knee-high boots I'm wearing scream "Club
Material," yet I can't help but feel awkward
and out of place. Hugging myself tight, I stand
in front of the club, uncertain if going in is the
right idea.

*I mean he said there are answers in
here, but what does that even mean?*

The fight inside me grows stronger as I
debate my next move. People glance at me
between puffs of their cigarettes, and my face

turns from a pasty white to a crimson red.

*Ugh, why am I always so friggin'
socially awkward?*

The pressure of eyes being on me, forces
my feet to move. My sweaty palm reaches for
the handle, as someone else's grabs it instead.
The strong male hand yanks the door open as I
run my eyes up his arm, to his face. Blinking a
few times, I see a handsome young man
standing with a crooked smile. His eyes are a
mesmerizing deep brown that I could get lost
in.

"After you," he gestures.

His voice is low, but not threatening.
Smiling like a fool, I proceed inside. A
bouncer stands at the door and my stomach
drops. I have no money and no way to prove
I'm old enough to get in.

*Gosh, why did I listen to Derrota? He
was just screwing around like his crazy
brother.*

The space is small, so I have no way of
turning around, but I know that I won't be able
to get inside. The eyes of the bouncer narrow

as I approach.

"I.D," he spits.

His tan arms are muscular and his tone is strict. The club is dark with the exception of a few strobes and black lights at the booths, but he can still see my face turn beet red. My eyes start darting around for a way out.

"Oh…Um, see… I—"

"She's with me," I hear from over my shoulder.

The guy who held the door open is close behind me. He lightly puts his hand on my shoulder, and my body melts a little. The bouncer continues staring at me with narrowed eyes.

"Put her on my tab, too," he says.

His hand on my shoulder pushes me forward a tad, guiding me into the club. A tinge of nervousness creeps up in my stomach, but I excuse it away as butterflies.

This dreamy guy wants me to go on his tab! No guy has ever even looked at me, let alone paid for me.

Soon, we're at a booth. The black light

illuminates the small space, showing all the graffitied names and obnoxious symbols on the table. He slides into the high backed booth and I follow suit on the other side. It's half-circle design sets us right next to each other as we watch the dance floor. People are letting the music flow through them like the alcohol in their systems.

For a moment, I forget I'm sitting next to this handsome guy, and lose myself in people watching. There's a woman in a cage to my far left who is dancing in barely any clothes. It's not exactly like the gentlemen's club Mary works at, but similar. In the middle of the crowd is a young girl with a very short, black and white dress on. As she turns, I see a touch of yellow in the front from a camisole, underneath hiding too much cleavage.

I wonder what it is that makes her feel so different from the busy people surrounding her. Her brown hair has streaks of blonde that were clearly dyed at home, and she's wearing clunky black shoes. As I study her, I notice that she's a little heavier. She's not as thin as some of the other girls I've met today, but not completely overweight either.

"You like what you see?"

My body jumps at the handsome guy's voice close to my ear.

"Oh, I'm sorry, what?"

He nods toward the girl with a hinting smile. "You like what you see?"

I look at him with furrowed eyebrows. "Uh—the dancing?"

Smiling with a chuckle he say, "The girl dancing…yeah."

"What?" I wrinkle my nose. "No! I mean she's pretty and all, but—no."

He puts his hands up in defense but the smile remains on his face. "Okay, sorry. You were just staring pretty hard at her and I wasn't sure if that meant—"

"It doesn't," I cut him off. "I just…I'm not sure. There's something about her that seems…"

"Sexy?" he grins.

"Ugh, no! God, what is wrong with you?" I groan. "Off. I was going to say 'there's something about her that seems off.' Perv."

The guy laughs.

"Listen, I'm sorry. I didn't mean to offend you." He strokes my arm with one of his fingers. "See, I just got back from deployment, so I have a few things I'd like to…explore, now that I'm back home."

I pull away from him. "Use that line much?" I ask sarcastically.

Scooching my way down doesn't seem to give this guy the hint. He continues to follow my body, trying to reach out and touch me again. Before I turn to slap him, a young African American girl steps in front of the table. She has her slender arms rested across her chest with one hip out.

"Adam, get the hell up on outta here," she demands. "Leave this poor girl alone."

"Cheyanne, we're just talkin', doll. No need to get jealous," Adam flirts back.

She turns to me. "Is he bothering you?"

I nod.

"Go away!" she yells back at him.

Adam makes his way around the table,

grumbling the whole time. Cheyanne looks him up and down with pursed lips and wide eyes as he goes toward another table. She slides in and sits across from me.

"Don't worry about him, honey. He's a sleaze ball that's always trying to get into every girls pants. Been there, done that, and did not buy the t-shirt because there was nothing to brag about."

I laugh. For what feels like the first time today, I'm honestly laughing at Cheyanne's joke. She smiles, but doesn't laugh back.

"So, it was a line then?" I ask.

"Him being deployed?"

"Yeah," I confirm.

"Nah, he really is in the military, but yes, he does use it to pick up ladies. He thinks girls like men in uniform better."

"He's probably right."

Turning my head back to the crowd I see the girl from before, up against the wall, making out with Adam. His hands are on places they shouldn't be, in public, and hers, draped over his neck. I cringe for her. He's so handsome, but also, such a jerk.

Hopefully a shot or two helped with that decision.

Cheyanne taps me on the hand, so I spin my head back quickly to meet her eyes.

"I said, do you want to dance?" she asks.

Wrinkling my face, I shake my head.

"Girl, I did not come out today to sit around. Do you know how long it took me to do my hair?"

She points to her bobbed haircut that is perfectly aligned to her face.

"Uh-uh, nope, we're going out and doing the damn thing."

My shoulders sag as Cheyanne drags me through the crowd to the dance floor. A popular song comes over the DJ's speakers. Everyone around me starts jumping up and down in excitement as my awkward self-starts swaying side to side. Cheyanne is dancing with some random guy while I bob my head, step to the right and left, and clap my hands.

"It's all in the hips."

The girl who was making out with

Adam pops up in front of me. Her breath reeks of alcohol and a small hickey on the curve of her neck. I cringe at the sight of it. While she starts dancing around me, trying to show me how to move my awkward body, I plaster a fake smile on my face.

"What's your deal? You're so stiff!" the girl yells over the music.

"Dancing just isn't my thing, at least not in public anyway," I shoot back. "I danced for eight years, but that was a long time ago."

"Hey! Me too!" she gleams.

I smile back. "Cool."

Grabbing my hand, she guides me off the dance floor and sits me back down at the booth from before. Secretly, I'm happy to be away from the chaos and awkwardness of the dance floor.

"Sorry, I need to sit for a minute," she huffs.

"No problem," I answer.

"You want a drink?"

"Oh, no, thanks though. I'm actually here to find my father. Have you seen an older man wearing a suit around? He's a little bald, and usually has a briefcase."

"What's your name?" the girl asks, ignoring my question.

"Savannah."

"Purdy."

"I'm sorry?" I ask leaning in.

"I'm Purdy!"

"I'm pretty?" I ask.

She laughs. "No, my name. It's Purdy!"

Laughing, I extend my hand. Purdy looks at it and wrinkles her forehead with a sarcastic smile.

"What are we, eighty?"

Slowly, I recoil my hand and place it back in my lap. Feeling a bright hue form on my cheeks, I look back out to the crowd dancing. Adam is on the dance floor making out with a different girl who is much thinner and prettier. I lean over to Purdy, still eyeing him.

"Doesn't that bother you?" I ask.

No answer comes and my heart skips a beat, knowing she's gone like the others.

Sheepishly, I look across the table. To my surprise, Purdy is still there, just sitting in silence. Watching her, I see that she's studying the girl as they dance with their hands all over each other.

A small tear falls from her done up lashes and she quickly wipes it away.

"Nah," she shrugs. "Guys will be guys, right?"

I furrow my brow at her. "Why are you upset? I mean, if he's just some guy…"

"Well," she says. "He's not just some guy…"

With confusion written all over my face, I lean further in.

"We used to go to school together," Purdy explains loudly. "I actually had a really big crush on him for a long time. Before he got deployed, he asked me to marry him…over messenger."

The two of us laugh.

"I know, stupid, right? But, I don't know, it was sweet. Then he went off and it turns out, he was seeing someone else…a lot of someone else's, actually. So, I had to let him go. Part of my heart is still attached to him, though. It's so dumb."

"No, that makes sense."

Purdy gestures as she gets up, so I follow. She walks up to the bar as I stand back. My nerves jump a little as I watch her order a drink.

She better not be getting one for me. I'm not about to be stumbling all over New York City.

I shift from my left foot to my right with my arms hugging my mid-section. Sweat is forming on my forehead from the lack of air in the club, so I roll my sleeves up forgetting about the welts that are spread across my skin.

Returning with one drink in her hand, she gestures for me to follow her again, and again, I comply. She heads toward the door going outside and as we walk, I stare at the blaring hickey on her neck.

Thankful, to be outside in the fresh air, I take a deep breath. Purdy places her beverage on the sidewalk near the wall, pulls a packet of cigarettes out of her bra along with a lighter, leans against the building, and lights up. She offers me a hit after she fills her lungs with polluted smoke.

"No, thank you," I politely decline.

The silence engulfs us as my ears adjust to the lack of booming music again. A chill runs up my spine from the winter breeze, so I pull my sleeves back down and try to guess the time.

The sun is still up, but it feels like it will be setting soon. Gosh, I have been running around all friggin' day.

My feet suddenly feel sore and my body droops a little from exhaustion.

"So," I break the awkwardness. "Why were you crying? I mean, I understand your story and all, but he seems like such a jerk. Isn't it better that you didn't get all caught up in that?"

"You're a straight shooter, aren't you?" Purdy asks with a chuckle.

I shrug. "Guess so. Curious is more like it."

Taking another long drag, Purdy narrows her eyes at me.

"My boyfriend just broke up with me. Like, this morning. I wasn't just crying over Adam, necessarily. I mean, yeah, he did break my heart. Just the fact that I can't keep a guy satisfied enough to love me is super annoying, ya know?"

"He just broke up with you, and you're already making out with someone?"

"Judge much?" Purdy flicks her cigarette before taking another drag.

"Sorry," I shake my head. "I didn't mean it to sound judgmental. I'm just surprised."

"Nah, I see you judging me with your judgy eyes." She exhales smoke. "I already told you, Adam isn't just 'someone.'"

She reaches down to grab her drink and stumbles a bit. I reach out to help her and she shoos me away. After drinking it all in one large gulp, she takes another drag from her stick of death and places the glass on the ground again.

"I swear, I'm not trying to judge. I just—"

"You say 'I' a lot, ever notice that?"

My mouth drops a little in shock.

"What?" I ask.

"Seems a bit self-centered, don't you think?"

"Whoa, okay, I'm just making conversation. You don't have to be like that."

She takes a drag, and flicks it before she exhales.

"Just sayin', has anyone ever told you that you're selfish?" she asks with a smirk.

"Once or twice," I admit. "Hasn't everyone been told that?"

Purdy shrugs. "Maybe."

Rolling my eyes, I look to my left.

Why am I even wasting my time here?

"Listen, Judgy McJudger, all I'll say is that when you feel empty inside, all you want to do is fill the void." Purdy hiccups. "Booze, drugs, sex, it's all the same…it all numbs the pain."

My eyes bulge out of my face.

"You're on drugs?" I whisper.

"Oh no, I'm just sayin'." She hiccups again. "When you're worthless, anything that numbs you does the trick."

"Don't say that about yourself, Purdy. You're not worthless."

Again, she narrows her eyes at me. "You don't know anything about me, Savannah. I could be the worst person you have ever met and you wouldn't even know."

"I'm sure you're not."

"Could have bodies in my basement, ever think of that?"

I take a cautious step back as she laughs.

"I'm not sayin' I do, I'm just sayin'; how would you know until it's too late? You shouldn't assume everyone is a good person just based off their looks."

"You shouldn't assume everyone is *bad* just based on their looks," I combat.

We stand in silence for quite a bit while I watch her puff more smoke into her lungs. I feel awkward from her constant narrowed eyes on me, and I'm scared to say too much.

"What exactly is bothering you?" Purdy asks suddenly.

Shrugging I answer, "I'm not entirely sure. I just don't really feel like myself today."

"Who are you?"

"What?" I ask wrinkling my forehead. "Who am I?"

"You said you don't feel like yourself today. So…who are you?"

Pondering this question, I bite the inside of my lower lip.

"I guess…I guess I don't really know. So much has happened, and it's made my brain a bit foggy. Am I the same person I was this morning? I honestly can't say."

Purdy shakes her head. "Nah, I don't accept that."

"Um—not sure it's for you to accept," I exhale sharply.

"Who are you?"

"No one special," I answer.

The sarcasm is starting to float it's way to the surface. It's my usual defense mechanism. This conversation is uncomfortable and annoying.

"That's really what you think of yourself?" Purdy asks peeling herself off the wall. She leans in toward me and her voice grows in volume. "Who. Are. You?"

"Gosh, would you stop asking me that! I don't know, okay? I don't know who I am. So much has happened to me and I've had to morph into people I never thought I would just to survive. I've had to do and be things no mother wants for their child. It's no wonder my parents hate me. It's no wonder I have no family. Who in God's name could love someone like me? Who am I? I'm a chameleon trying to blend into the background and skate through life!"

The door burst open, and Cheyanne comes stumbling out of the building. For a short moment, the air is filled with another rap song. A huge smile is spread across her drunk face. I raise my eyebrows as she drapes a long arm around my neck for support.

"Smoking without me, huh? What kind of friend are you?"

I shake my head. "No, I'm not, Purdy is—"

Once again, the girl I've been conversing with is gone without a trace. Part of me is relieved. I hate losing my temper like that. The other part of me is frustrated.

This must be my new normal. I conclude. *At this point, I'm just talking to myself.*

Walking Cheyanne over to the building, I lower her down to sit on the ground.

"I'm sorry, I have to go." I tell her. "Will you be okay out here?"

Cheyanne reaches into my cleavage and pulls out the pack of cigarettes that Purdy had. She taps the box with her lighter as I stare in awe at what just happened.

"I'm good," she says.

Standing straight up, I look down and see that I'm in the same skin tight outfit that Purdy had on. My body feels too big for something too small and the heels strapped to my feet are making my aching feet throb more.

Taking a deep breath and fighting tears I begin to walk away from the shotty club.

Here we go again…

-Chapter Fourteen-

Clearly, there *were no answers there*. I sigh in frustration. *What a shock, the Goorin brother lead me to a dead end.*

As I follow the crowd in an unknown direction, I get a glimpse of myself in the windows passing by. Stopping, I study myself. Lowering my eyebrows and scrunching up my cheek, I sigh heavily. I don't even recognize the reflection I'm looking at in the blacked out window. The face is the same, yes, but the dress, hair, heels, and make-up are all from Purdy. Even the small hickey on the small of my neck made me cringe.

"Who are you?" Purdy's voice fills my head.

Staring at this person makes my stomach drop. I touch my face dramatically and slide my fingertips down my jaw line while choking back tears once again.

Who am I?

There's a slight scar on the top of my right eyebrow from when I got stitches as a kid. The details of my face are coming together for the first time. My large nose and sad, round eyes take up most of my face. With a hand still on the side of my face, I watch the tears fall.

Who are you? Purdy's voice echoes.

Am I really myself? Or am I just a version of myself? Do we stay the same from birth to coffin, or is the whole point to grow and evolve? If I evolve, does that make me different or the same? Is that who I was always meant to be or who I became based on my situation? Is it a good thing or a bad thing and how do we truly ever know?

Questions float through my head with no answers and no sign of resolution. I feel someone's hand lightly on my shoulder. I look to my right and see a face I don't recognize. He smiles at me as if he's holding back laughter. I smile back with wide eyes not getting the joke.

"You do know you're staring right into a restaurant, right?" he asks.

The smile drops from my face and it turns beet red.

"Uh—what?"

"Yeah, like right into our booth," he says. This time laughter follows. "The window looks like it's blacked out, but there's people inside watching you."

My mouth goes dry and without a word, I take off running, his laughter still in my ears.

This isn't happening. This isn't happening. I can't escape self-sabotaging moments even in a reality that I don't understand.

The heels on my feet hurt so badly, so when I know it's a safe distance from my humiliation, I stop and take them off. Some people give me a strange look, but it's been a long day. I give them a dead, side-eyed glance and they quickly move on.

Waiting at a large intersection, I finally gather that I'm at Central Park. This information does nothing for me because I have no idea how to get back to Port Authority, but at least I am near something that makes sense. Bouncing from one foot to the other while the light is at a standstill, I see the image of my father on the other side.

There's no way, I tell myself with my eyes wide.

His balding head and suit are too hard to miss and once the light changes to green, I sprint toward him determined not to lose him again. I dodge between people, knocking into a few of them. My fingers hold tight to Purdy's heels as I race to the other side of the long crosswalk. My heart beats wildly as I watch my father take a call on his cell and walk into Central Park.

Gaining speed from the adrenaline coursing through my veins, I huff in amazement that he seems to only be getting further away.

No, I curse under my breath. *No! How is that possible?*

The feeling of being on a treadmill with a Twinkie dangling in front of it comes to mind for some reason. My legs run faster, but I watch as the distance grows like an optical illusion. The people and space around me warps like I'm in a tunnel.

Finally, he stops on the sidewalk deep in the park. I'm breathing heavily, but refusing to give in to my weakness. Making my way over the stone bridge, I know that I can get to him if I just keep going.

"Just keep going," I hear the man say. For a moment I smell his coffee and cigarette breath as if he's here with me. Knowing in all reality, that he will always be with me in spirit.

"Dad!" I yell. "Stop, Dad, it's me!"

I wave my arm like a lunatic trying to get his attention, when suddenly I'm knocked to the ground. Someone pushes me, sending me straight to the concrete. A band of runner's nearly tramples me as I inch my body away from under their giant, pounding feet.

"Ugh!" I groan.

"Oh you poor thing," I hear. "I saw the whole thing and rushed over."

The scratchy voice belongs to a homeless teen who is bending down to help me up. She grabs my arm and we both pull my body off the cold ground.

"There ya go," she smiles.

I dust my bottom off with my eyes still on the girl. Even though she's smiling, her eyes are filled with sadness. This concept is perplexing to me, and it draws me to her in a way I can't explain.

"Um, thank you…" I hesitate.

The girl is around my age, looking to be a few years younger. This places a pit in my stomach. Being so close in age, yet in such different stages of our lives makes me uncomfortable and nervous for some reason.

"I'm Savannah." I extend my hand.

She takes it lightly into her cold palm and shakes it.

"Glad to meet you," she says properly. "My name is Roxanna, but people just call me

Roxie."

For an awkward moment, we stand silently shaking each other's hands.

"You must be cold," Roxie says. She shrugs off her lightly torn sweater and hands it to me. "Here, take this."

I hesitate. Taking clothes from people I don't know always makes me uncomfortable. Goodwill is great, but not when it comes to clothes and couches. Roxie sees me pause and chuckles.

"It's actually clean," she says.

Guilt floods my body and I quickly take the sweater. Pulling my arms through and zipping it halfway, I smell the soft scent of lavender. It's warm like it's fresh out of the dryer and my body relaxes a bit. I feel more normalized being in a hoodie, a clean hoodie at that.

"I'm sorry, I didn't mean to offend."

"Oh, no," Roxie shrugs it off. "It's okay. I would have wondered the same thing."

"Is it too forward to ask if I can buy you something to eat?" I offer.

Immediately I regret this decision.

You have no money, moron.

Roxie smiles but shakes her head. "I couldn't accept that. Thank you, though."

There's a poking in my bra that is driving me nuts, so I turn my body away a little and reach into it. Expecting a pack of smokes to be lodged where Purdy had stored them, I feel around. To my surprise, it's not the carton, but a crisp twenty dollar bill.

You can't use that…it's not yours. I tell myself. *Well, then maybe Purdy should have kept her clothes on!* I argue with…myself.

Holding up the money I say, "A hot dog or maybe a pretzel? I'm actually really hungry myself."

Roxie opens her mouth to decline politely again, but I lightly grab her hand before she gets a chance to deny me. We walk down the path, away from where I had been trampled on and I see a cart close ahead. Trying not to seem too crazy, I let go of her hand and join her side at a normal pace.

She smiles again and says, "I didn't

always look like this, you know."

I overly act like I have no idea what she's talking about by widening my eyes and shaking my head.

"I'm not sure what you mean."

Roxie laughs at my obvious attempt to treat her normally.

"The gesture is appreciated, but we can both acknowledge that I'm homeless."

I shrug with a slight smile as we approach the hot dog stand.

"What can I get you ladies," the vendor asks.

He eyes Roxie not so subtly and I see her shy away in my peripheral vision. Clearing my throat and acting like I'm looking the cart over, I attempt to gain his attention.

"Let's see…" I say nonchalantly. "We'll have two hot dogs with everything and two bottles of water."

"That'll be sixteen even," he says.

Gotta love the city…

I hand him the only money I have to my name at this moment and watch as he counts four dollars back. I gesture toward the tip cup, and he grins while placing it inside. Silently, we wait as the vendor makes up our meals while he whistles a tune. He hands Roxie the hot dog and water first.

"Thanks, have a good day," I say as I take the food from him.

There's a bench next to the stand, so we make our way over. Roxie is stiff, probably from the sadness of me having to pay for her. She places the water next to her on the seat and pulls a small piece of the bun off. A young white man rushes over to us once we are situated on the benches. He's holding a handful of flyers in one hand and a few CD's in the other.

"Hey, ladies!" he greets. "I'm MC Whyte Rabit, comin' at cha with a hot new track straight out of the studio."

I roll my eyes.

"Would you fine ladies be interested in this single?"

Shaking my head, I say, "Nah, thank you though."

"We just used our money on food. Maybe next time…" Roxie says politely.

"Ah, cool, cool. I hear ya. Well, hey," he extends his arm with the fliers. "Take one of these and mark it on your calendar. I'll be droppin' some beats at a club a few blocks from here this weekend."

As I begin to shake my head, I see Roxie extend her arm and take the neon green piece of paper with a smile.

"You ladies have a great day now," he says.

He rushes off to another group of people standing by and I look at Roxie. She takes the paper, folds it in half, and places it under her leg so it doesn't fly away.

"That was very kind of you, thank you," she says sheepishly.

"What was?" I ask.

My mind is so fixated on my growling stomach.

Roxie giggles. "The food."

Diving into my hot dog I say, "No problem."

While I chew and try to settle my raging stomach, Roxie picks at hers slowly.

Maybe she's trying to make it last by taking her time. I think. *Not me.* Taking another bite, I sigh.

"So," I say out of the side of my mouth. "If you don't mind me asking, what happened?"

Roxie nibbles a small piece of bread.

"I was kicked out," she sniffles.

"Kicked out?" I ask horrified. "How old are you?"

Roxie rubs her nose with the back of her long sleeved shirt. Then she wipes the tears away with the palm of her hand.

Clearing her throat, she says, "Uh—eighteen."

-Chapter Fifteen-

My mouth drops mid-chew.

"Eighteen?"

Roxie nods. "Yeah." She chuckles softly. "I had a good family. We had our problems, ya know, but who doesn't?"

She places another small piece of bread into her mouth before continuing.

"My mom worked hard. My step-father was nice and he taught me a lot about things: politics, religion, and baseball. He had so many books and, if I was really careful with them, sometimes I could take them into my room and read."

The water bottle crinkles as I sip from it.

"Oops, sorry," I say.

"Eventually, they had a baby together," she continues without acknowledging the sound. "My whole life, I prayed for a baby brother. I would look for the brightest star and wish for him to come into my life. God finally answered that prayer."

She paused.

"I love him so much." She sniffles again. "Do you have siblings?"

Opening my mouth to answer, my mind goes blank. "Uhh—"

"Well, I can tell you," she continues, "there's nothing like having a younger sibling, especially one that you have been asking for."

She takes a deep, shaky breath.

"After my brother was born, the house shifted. Everything changed. It was no longer the three of *us.* It was now the three of *them.* They would do things to exclude me at first. Movies, eating out as a family, or grocery shopping. I mean, I get it, I was in high school. I should have been able to take it…but… it was still painful to be left out. I felt like they didn't want me around."

I finish off my hot dog because I have no self-control, but continue to listen intensely.

"It was really hard sometimes. I already felt like I wasn't wanted or loved. Then I finally have this little family and it vanished. Just…poof, gone."

"Do you resent your brother?" I ask.

"God no!" Roxie exclaims. "No way. He was just stuck in the middle. I could never blame him or resent him."

I nod. She continues to pick at the food, but doesn't eat it.

"I clung to my small group of friends and eventually a boyfriend. They were the only ones who made me feel like…like I had worth. Earlier this year, when I was still seventeen, my step-father told me I had to leave. I wasn't allowed to stay after high school was over, which was only a few months away."

She rubs her sweaty palm on her dirty sweatpants.

"Well, your mom couldn't have been

okay with that. I mean, where would you go?"

Roxie nods slowly, but doesn't say anything. I watch as a tear drips from her lashes and lands on her shirt.

"I ended up living with my boyfriend and his parents. Gosh they were so nice to me. His mom even insisted that I called her mom. She was livid at my family for kicking me out. I really miss them a lot…but they have a really bad drug problem. I couldn't stay there…"

Listening to this sounds like I'm listening to a telenovela and my heart breaks for her.

"My ex's mother went over the border to smuggle drugs into the states. It was so scary because she didn't even tell us about it. I mean, I guess that's a good thing in hindsight, but at the time, we didn't know what happened to her. We were calling everyone we could, trying to figure out if she was okay."

I wipe my mouth with a napkin as Roxie continues to dish out all this crazy information.

"I remember his father was on the phone with hospitals because he was scared that she got hurt…but then we got a call from her. She was in jail over the border and wasn't sure when she would be let go."

Roxie wipes her nose again.

"I was so relieved that she was okay, but at the same time, I was so pissed. I know we needed money…but that?"

Shaking my head I say, "Whoa, that's no joke…how did she even get out of a situation like that?"

Taking a deep breath, she continues. "I don't know a lot of the details between that phone call and her coming home. She said she didn't want to talk about it, so we didn't. But…"

Roxie pauses. I sit eagerly waiting for more.

"After she came home…there was this really weird van that would sit outside of our apartment. Day and night, it was just…sitting. The windows were completely blacked out and it wasn't in a parking spot, ya know. Like, it was facing forward as if it was about to take off at any minute.

Eventually, his mother somehow found out through her community of people, again I didn't ask questions, that it was the FBI. Like, the *real* FBI was stationed outside of our apartment. They followed her when she left and stayed for…gosh, I don't even know how long, but a long time."

My mouth hangs open. "No way, that can't be right."

Sighing and sagging her shoulders, Roxie says, "That's what I said, but as far as I was told, it was true. I honestly have no way to confirm or deny it. All I know is *someone* was sitting outside of our apartment and following her around. Honestly," she says. "I hope it was the FBI, because if it wasn't…I don't even want to think of what could have happened to us."

"Oh my gosh…so how did you end up leaving?"

"Well, it wasn't until I found a meth pipe in our house that I said I was done. My ex and I were at the end of our relationship anyway, so it was just time…"

"Did you go back to your parents?" I ask.

"I went home for a quick few days before I was told I had to leave again. So…I've been couch surfing. Staying with friends here and there. I'm actually about to move in with an old teacher of mine from high school. His wife and kids are the sweetest and offered for me to live there in exchange for babysitting sometimes."

Roxie breaks out into a full on sob. I wrap my arm around her and try to comfort her. Tears are building up in my own eyes as I watch this poor teenager suffer emotionally.

"I just don't get it, ya know?" she asks.

"Get what?"

She sniffs back more tears.

"I don't get how total strangers can take me in, care for me, love me, and yet my own parents can't."

"What happened to your mom?" I ask again. "She just let you go?"

Roxie doesn't answer right away. Tears just fall down her cheeks, making lines on her face.

"I don't know why she allowed this to happen to me. Sometimes, I wonder why I even bother. I know I wasn't a perfect kid. I know I argued a lot and I would stay out late. I know that I spent a lot of time in my room, but no one cared and I felt that. I knew that staying out until ten or eleven wouldn't matter. It didn't happen often but when it did, no one questioned it. Their careless attitude just caused me to lash out more because, God, some attention was better than none at all. I felt like a ghost in my own home!"

I wipe my nose with her sweater.

"My parents don't love me, I have no home… why do I even keep going?" she asks.

Grabbing the unused napkins from the vendor, I place one on my lap and offer the other to Roxie.

"Here."

She takes it with a forced smile but doesn't look me in the eyes.

"Thanks."

We both blow our noses at the same

time.

"I'm so sorry, this is so inappropriate. I just met you, and here you are buying me food and listening to my sob story…"

"Please, don't. It's okay, I really don't mind."

She wipes her wet eyes.

"I wish there was something I could do to help you. I just moved in with family myself, so there isn't much I could offer."

Roxie gives a sad chuckle. "That's very kind of you, but I won't do that anyway. It's bad enough I'm like this, let alone, for me to burden a perfect stranger."

Clearing my throat, I ask, "What about other family members?"

She chuckles lightly. "I have some people I could ask, but mostly everyone has their own stuff going on, ya know? I don't think I would necessarily be turned away by people, but I know I would be a burden on their lives. Living with an ex-teacher is hard enough to come to terms with. I feel like I am a constant burden on his family."

Roxie looks at me quickly.

"It's not that they have ever said that or alluded to it. I just feel like I am. How could I not be, really. They are taking in this troubled teen who has little to nothing to her name and her parents don't even care. How could that not feel burdensome?"

She wipes her nose again while I think about the immense pressure she must be under. The fact that she has to figure out life at such a young age is hard to understand. None of her family knows how low she's gotten, and that has to hurt almost as bad as her parents not caring enough to ask.

A shiver runs up my spine as the warmth of the sun hides behind some buildings. Biting my lip, I watch the goosebumps spread across my bare legs.

"I really think you should try to talk to your mother again, Roxie. I know she's busy, and might even have a lot going on in her own life, but you're her daughter. That has to count for something, right?"

I hear her sad chuckle. As another shiver

crosses my body, I wait for her to counter my statement. When nothing comes, I decide to put my arm around her. As I lean my body over with my arm extended, there is nothing but space. Catching myself on the bench, my lips part.

But of course... I shake my head.

Another chill runs up my back, this time from the creepy sensation filling my body.

No matter how many times this happens, I can't get used to it.

Annoyed, I stand up. Someone comes over in a huff as I begin to leave. She breezes past me before leaning down to pick up the nibbled hot dog on the ground. With a dramatic toss into the garbage can, she turns to glare at me.

"There's a trash can right here! What's your problem?" she demands.

Her arms are crossed and her hip is sticking out as she leans to her right side, tapping her foot.

"I'm sorry, I didn't mean to leave it..."

Without warning her face drops along

with her stern posture. She seems to be instantly softening.

"No, no," she insists. "I shouldn't have—" Reaching into her pocket, she says, "Here, please, take some money."

Backing up with my hands in the air, I shake my head.

"Oh my gosh, no, I couldn't. Thank you, though, it's very kind of you."

"It's not much, but it's something."

The woman charges forward and places the folded bills into my palm, careful not to touch me. Quickly, she runs off into a crowd of people. Looking down to find a place to put the money, I see that I'm wearing the dirty sweatpants that Roxie had on. My shoes have changed too, from a heel to a ratty old sneaker that used to be white.

Groaning, I shove the money into my, Roxie's, sweater pocket. Turning back in the direction I was headed before the girl rushed over, I begin to walk away from the confusing scene.

This has to all make sense soon, right?

Maybe my aunt can explain it to me…if she's even real. Am I really doubting my aunt? The one person who's been there for me? Her and Uncle D have done more for me than anyone I know…yet I'm questioning them? This really must be some kind of dream…

-Chapter Sixteen-

With no clear idea where I'm headed, I manage to move one foot in front of another. Even though I'm comfortable in these new clothes, the fact that I'm wearing them is still a little freaky. The weight of the day is heavy on me, and I can't seem to shake this constant heaviness.

Glancing around, I try to find a hint of my father somewhere. At this point, if I don't find him, I don't know what to do. Port Authority is far, and I honestly don't even know where to begin without my aunt's experienced knowledge to guide me.

Craning my neck over my left shoulder, I see the same figure as before in a long black coat standing not too far behind me. Instantly, I feel a surge of fear rush through my body. Again, I can't see the person's face and I don't like being alone in a place where I'm vulnerable. My speed quickens in hopes to create distance between us.

As I rush farther into Central Park, the figure is still close by. It actually feels as if it's closer now. My heart pumps as I quickly suck in cold air. The figure is looming over me. I can almost feel it's breath on the back of my neck.

"Help!" I yell. "Someone help me!"

There's a crowd of people surrounding me, but no one seems to notice my cries for help. A pair of familiar faces are right in front of me, but I can't place them. Two ladies talk amongst themselves, one is greatly older, the other about half her age. Their features are similar, yet different, as if they are related.

"Hey!" I cry. "Over here! Please, someone's after me!"

My cries aren't heard by them. They aren't heard by anyone. People pass by my distress with little to no care, as I run for my life.

What's going to happen if this person catches me? Oh, God, please help me!

As if in slow motion, I feel long, slender fingers grip my shoulder. With a hard yank, I pull myself free, but the fingers get caught in my hair. My head gets thrown back cracking my bones loudly. With all my might, I pull my body forward, escaping the claws, and sending my uncontrollable force into a young girl on the running trail.

Smacking right into her, I send us both flying to the ground. Quickly, I scramble to my feet, and turn around to face the scary, mysterious person, but no one's there. People are whispering as they pass me, clearly talking about my unstable mental health. With a red face and unsteady hand, I reach down to help the young lady I pummeled.

"Gosh, I'm so sorry," I apologize. "Someone was chasing me and I didn't see you."

As she dusts herself off, she says, "Don't worry about it. Accidents happen. I wasn't really paying attention to where I was going anyway."

Keeping a cautious eye out for the perpetrator, I scan the crowd.

"Yeah, my mind is just about everywhere else but here," I state.

When I'm satisfied that the coast is clear, I look at the girl. Her honey blonde hair is pulled back into a messy bun that sits on top of her head. She was clearly out for some exercise in her black yoga pants and black, pink, and white jogging jacket. The hot pink running shoes stands out boldly from the rest of the outfit. Her frame isn't as slender as I would have thought for a runner, but who am I to judge?

She gives a faint smile and extends her hand. "I'm Leah."

Accepting her kindness, I say, "Nice to meet you, Leah. I'm Savannah."

"That's a beautiful name," she says,

starting to walk in the direction I was escaping toward.

"Are you a runner?" I ask. "I always wanted to be a runner, but I could never last longer than a couple days."

Leah chuckles. "It's definitely a lot of work and takes a ton of motivation. Sometimes I just don't want to get out of bed, but I have to push myself so I can get through the day. If I can finish a run, I can tackle anything the day has in store for me."

My eyes widen at the statement.

"Wow, I love your grit. I honestly wish I was like that. The idea of exercise always sounds great the night before, but then the alarm goes off and I think, eh, is being an arbuckle that big of a deal?"

"A what?" Leah laughs.

I shake my head with a smile. "Nothing…just an inside joke."

The joke is there, but I can't quite remember where I've heard it from. Like a faint memory from another life. Right on the edge of your brain but just far enough out of reach. For a brief moment, it feels like I'm empty inside…like part of my soul is missing from my body.

Leah's voice snaps me away from this weird, awkward feeling of loneliness.

"Do you ever feel like you just want to run away?" Leah asks. "Like everything is so screwed up that you just don't want to go on anymore?"

With her hands in her pockets, she sighs, throws her head back and closes her eyes.

"I—certainly have at various points of my life. There were times where I question if life is even worth living - when the pain of what I've done is just too heavy to carry anymore."

"Exactly," she chokes back tears. "That's why I run. I pretend like I'm going somewhere far away, much farther than Central park. I imagine I'm going somewhere I can start over, cut all ties so no one knows who I am. Even though, I know at the end of my run I'm still stuck here. Putting in my headphones and imagining I'm in a magical place that no one knows me keeps me going, though."

Leah glances over to me with a crimson face. "Ugh, I'm so sorry. I'm just spewing all this on you and we don't even know each other."

"Oh, please, don't even worry about it. After the day I've been having, this is nothing." I smile. "I just have a trustworthy face, I guess."

She smiles sadly. "Yeah, you do."

Clearing my throat, I ask, "What are you running from exactly? Or is that, like, way too personal?"

After a long pause, I glance at Leah out of the corner of my eye. I see tears sliding down her face and she sniffles back more. Before I can correct my forward question, her lips part.

"Myself…" she whispers.

Not sure what to say, I stare at the ground. The constant sniffles signal to me that Leah hasn't vanished into thin air like the other girls which makes me confident in the silence.

So many questions flood my brain, but I want to respect her space as well.

"I thought…I thought I could finally have it, ya know?" she finally says. "Someone who cared about me like their very own. Someone who would walk me down the aisle on my wedding day or grill my boyfriend to make sure he was worthy of me…" Her voice breaks.

Tears well up in my eyes. No attempt of stopping would help because she is hitting a note that I have felt for as long as I can remember. The pain of wanting to be loved, but having no one there to love you.

"He had other plans, though. God, I should have seen the signs! It had happened once before and I knew…I knew it was too good to be true," she blurts out.

"What was, Leah?" I ask.

"Having a father." She begins to sob. "He said he cared about me like a father. That he had my picture up in his office from when I was a little girl and even though we weren't in contact, he thought of me like his daughter. He told me stories about how my mother kept him in the loop about the going on's in my life. When I succeeded, which wasn't often, and when I failed, which was all the time."

"Who are we talking about here. I'm so sorry to interrupt, I'm just super confused."

Leah is hyperventilating as the tears roll down her face. With shameful eyes she looks deep into mine and shakes her head.

"Where do I begin?"

-Chapter Seventeen-

Leah is crying hard, but is still able to speak through her tears. My eyes are stinging from trying not to show my emotions too much. The weight of the day is still hanging heavily on me and my eyelids are failing to remain fully open. I'm mentally, physically, and emotionally drained from today's, events and I'm ready to just curl up and take a long nap in a quiet corner.

"I guess at the beginning," I shrug.

"Well," she gasps. "If I start at the beginning, I'll have to tell you about my uncle…are you sure you want to go down that road?"

Blinking a few times, I nod. "You seem like you really need to talk to someone and I'm a very good listener. So, whatever you want to share is up to you."

She narrows her eyes at me. "Why are you even here anyway?"

"That, love, is the million dollar question."

Leah chuckles a little. "I mean, in Central Park. You said someone was chasing you?"

Nodding again, I say, "Yeah, someone was, but I don't know who, and trust me, I am keeping an eye out." I exhale. "Honestly, Leah, I have no idea what's going on and I need the distraction if you need a shoulder to cry on. This day has been one that I can't even begin to explain."

She smiles lightly and nods. Taking a deep breath, she steers me toward a bench.

"I have to sit down…" she says.

Looking around to make sure no creepers are in the bushes, I take a seat next to

Leah. She clears her throat, the sobbing subsiding for now, and begins.

"So…my uncle has always been a little strange. I didn't know him too well when I was little. He wasn't around much, but I always knew about him. I grew up in a family that basically talked about everyone behind their backs, so I heard stories I probably shouldn't have at a very young age. Despite that, he was always very nice to me. He would play video games with me and teach me how to play the harder ones, like Tomb Raider."

I smile remembering the horrible graphics of that game on my PlayStation when it first came out.

"He even lived with us for a little while. His bedroom was next to mine, but I don't remember him being home a lot."

Picking at the loose string on her jacket, I see tears welling up again.

"One day, my mom and I were at my other uncle's house. We'll call him 'Uncle B.' She was upstairs and I was downstairs with my aunt and my cousins. Uncle "A" came over and went right up to talk to my mother…all I remember was he stormed down the stairs, almost broke Uncle B's front door, and sped off right away. His stuff was gone when we went home the next day and no one really talked about it."

I inhale sharply.

"For weeks after he left, I remember he would come to our house late at night and bang on the door. It didn't happen often, maybe just a few times, but that was enough to really frighten my mom. See, I had this big window in my room that looked out to the front of the house. There was a cute little ledge that you could sit on and read or whatever. I remember for a long time my mom would sit there through the night with a big kitchen knife in her hand."

Gasping, I place my hand over my mouth.

"Oh my gosh," I whisper.

"Yeah, it was pretty scary. Not even really because of him, if you'll believe it. I honestly didn't know what was going on. It was scary because my mom was scared. There's something about seeing a parent in fear that makes a child even more on edge than they would normally be."

I nod, my hand still over my mouth.

"Anyway, fast forward some years, maybe like seven? I was fourteen and… developing…" Leah gestures to her chest. "I told you this was going to be awhile," she laughs.

Chuckling I say, "I honestly don't mind."

She smiles and continues.

"For whatever reason I was allowed to go over to his house by that point. He had married and his wife was always very nice to me. I was allowed to spend time there and spent the night occasionally. In all honesty, I was never super comfortable there, but I didn't know how to say no when they asked if I wanted to come over, so I just went.

One day he picked me up early before his wife had gotten home, and we were playing a video game, like usual. A very busty woman character comes on screen and my uncle looks at my chest and says, 'Doesn't even come close.' Then looks back at the screen and proceeds to play the game…"

My mouth drops. "What?"

She nods. "Yeah, it was super uncomfortable, but I wasn't sure what to think about it. Like was it a joke I just didn't understand? Did I misunderstand what he did and where he was looking? It was all very confusing."

Leah takes another shaky breath.

"Then one night when I was staying over, he was out with some work people and it was just his wife and I. It was late, so I fell asleep on the couch, where I would sleep when I was there. I woke up in the middle of the night, and he was sitting on the ottoman in front of me just…watching me. Like, literally, just sitting in the darkness, watching me sleep. It was so scary. He shushed me back to sleep and rubbed my head for a little before eventually going into his room for the night. So many things were rolling around in my brain. Did he do that often? How long had he been there? *Why* was he there? There was no sleeping that night. I was so freaked out that I couldn't fall back asleep, and the next day I told them I wasn't feeling well so I could go home early."

She pauses for a moment to let the stories sink in. Quietly, I wait, trying to make sense of all that has happened to this young lady. This alone was horrific to live through…and then she continues.

"Progressively it got worse. It went from weird looks to actual touching. He would slap my butt a lot, but I noticed, not when other people were around. For example, I stayed with my grandparents in their cabin for the summer in high school. Him and his wife came the last week I was there and I was supposed to fly back with them. The two of us where playing pool downstairs in the basement and they called us up for dinner, so he ushered me to go first. I hesitated, but he insisted, 'ladies first,' so I tried to quickly go up the stairs. The problem was, I wasn't quick enough and he slapped my butt the whole way to the top, but stopped right before I opened the door where everyone was."

My eyes widen at this.

"Why didn't you tell him to stop?" I ask.

Leah inhales sharply. "Well, I had told my mom that he made me uncomfortable and that he would occasionally touch my butt. She brushed it off and just said, 'he's weird.' Because of her reaction to it, I felt like I was making a big deal out of nothing. I mean, when you go to your mother and she doesn't seem to be upset about it, what else are you supposed to do? Yell at him in front of everyone and have all of them say how ridiculous you sound? It was a confusing situation because I didn't like the contact, but no one seemed too concerned."

Shaking my head, I look at the foliage in front of us. The weight of this conversation is heavy and honestly hard to comprehend.

Why would her mother allow her around him when she had to sit at the window with a knife because of him? Let alone after all this

uncomfortable contact and whatever happened
at Uncle B's house.

"Then, when I moved out—"

"There's more?" I ask.

"I'm sorry, you're right, I should shut up about all this."

"Oh my gosh, no," I quickly say. "I just mean, that is all hard enough to go through, how could there be more?"

Leah smiles faintly. "We've only just begun."

-Chapter Eighteen-

Sucking in a cold breath, I brace myself for what could possibly be coming at me now.

"When I moved out, I tried really hard to keep my distance from him. I ended up living with a girl from my high school and by this point his wife had given birth to their son. They insisted on coming over to see the place and I had run out of excuses so, to my house they came. That time wasn't bad honestly. We played Guitar Hero and had lunch. The baby was so sweet, so I enjoyed seeing him. They left and I felt like my quota was filled.

Later that week, I got a phone call from my uncle saying that he wanted to come over to help me with my broken laptop. I had totally forgotten that in the awkward lack of conversation with them, I had mentioned that it wasn't working right. He was very insistent, so I finally caved. The next day, him and his baby came over. He set up the Pack 'n Play, placed him in and…"

Tears stream down Leah face and her lip quivers. She's staring at the ground and I can just imagine that this whole scene is playing out in her head again.

"That's okay, Leah. You can stop…"

"No," her voice shakes. "No, I need to get this out. I need to be heard!"

I nod, but she doesn't see.

"He placed him in the Pack 'n Play and sat on the couch next to me. I sat as far away from him as I could, but he sat so close our legs touched. Then he began to talk about how he hadn't been…intimate with his wife because of the pregnancy. I nodded and listened because I didn't know what to do…then he asked…"

Leah put her face in her hands signaling to me that this is way harder than I could imagine for one person to carry.

"He asked if he could touch my breasts…" she begins to sob. "I didn't say no, Savannah. I didn't say no because I was scared. Before I knew it, he had moved me in between his legs facing away from him, unzipped my hoodie, and was…was just…"

She can't say the words.

He molested her…oh my God…he molested her.

My mouth is dry as tears stream down my face for her. I want to place my arm around her shoulders to comfort her as she sobs, but I don't want to touch her in fear she will get freaked out, so I sit helplessly.

"I felt… him… on my back. His breath was on my neck. He leaned his forehead on the back of my head, and I knew that if I didn't get up he would do something much worse than… So, I stood and said I had to go to school. Little did he know I had dropped out of College in order to work to pay the bills, but that was the first thing that came to mind. I ran upstairs, paced for about ten minutes, changed, and slowly made my way downstairs. He was finishing packing up his son, who had been watching the whole time, and we all walked out. Then he insisted on filling my gas tank for some weird reason and we parted ways."

"Oh, God…" My mind is too foggy for anything more than that.

"He took my laptop, so I had to get it back the next week. That was awkward, but not terrible like the time before that. I quickly stopped by, told him I had to pick up a friend of mine at school, and the worst he did was hug me way too long so 'our heart beats would synch up' and then I left. Thank God that was the last time I saw him."

"I am so sorry, Leah. This is so terrible, and I'm devastated you had to go through this."

Tears formed in both our eyes.

"I'm telling you all this because I should have seen the signs. I should have *known* that something bad was about to happen. I truly should have been able to stop it, ya know. But I didn't. I didn't speak up, I didn't know what to do. It took me a whole month to even tell anyone what happened because I was so ashamed and conflicted, like it was my fault somehow."

"But it wasn't your fault! You told your mom early on. You tried to distance yourself from him. You were cautious when you were around him. Even if you didn't do any of those things, it *still* wouldn't be your fault. *He* crossed a line. *He* abused your trust in him."

Leah's lips part and she looks at me sadly. "But I didn't say no…that's the first question that the police officer's ask when you're finished reporting it. 'Why didn't you say no?' Followed closely with, 'Why did it take you so long to report this.' I was ashamed and they made me feel even more like it was my fault. Luckily, my mom was there for me that time. She went down to the station and then courthouse with me so I wasn't alone…that time."

My eyes narrow suspiciously. "What do you mean, 'that time?'"

A sad chuckle escapes through Leah's tears. "I told you that was only the beginning."

I close my eyes trying to steady my shaking body, processing her words.

"Jesus," I whisper closing my eyes.

-*Chapter Nineteen*-

"The reason I told you that is because it's important information to know for what I'm about to tell you. The two are…connected in a way that's still hard to understand. It's still a tough story for me to get out, so…bear with me, okay?" Leah asks, but doesn't look me in the eye.

I nod, biting the inside of my lip from the anticipation of what's to come.

"There's no judgment here, Leah. I promise."

She nods gnawing on her bottom lip. "That's what everyone says…"

"Well, this time it's true."

We both take a deep breath almost in unison, and she begins.

"When I was a little girl, my mother had a husband. He wasn't very nice and from what I remembered of him, he wasn't very good. He hit her, a lot, and did bad things to me. He hit me with belts, locked me in my closet and left the apartment, that sort of thing. He even punched a hole through the wall once while he was fighting with my mom."

Leah pauses. I adjust on the uncomfortable bench and wrap my arms around my midsection.

"A little off topic, but I can recall this one time that my mom was trying to leave him. We got up really early in the morning. It wasn't even fully light outside yet, and she was buckling me in the car seat. I kept asking where's 'daddy,' because that was what I was supposed to call him, and she continued to shush me. Then I remember she turned around in the front seat, and he was standing in front of the car in his boxers. I don't remember what happened after that, but I know she stayed with him, so I can only imagine what events took place once we were inside."

She clears her throat.

"Anyway, that just goes to show you how we lived. After they got divorced, I didn't know they had contact. I lived in fear of him, and my mother knew what he had done to me, so I thought he was just a part of our past that we *never* talked about. Anytime I would bring up that he hit her or how scared I was she would tell me that it never happened…but I knew—I *know*, it did. For a long time, I felt crazy because for *years* she would tell me that I was fed the information or I was remembering it wrong. Until I was in high school and my step-father at the time confirmed that she told him it did happen. She lied to me for years because she was ashamed…

I get that, I do, but man, was that a punch in the gut. This fear of someone that I thought was out of our lives being shoved under the rug like that: it's one of those things that you know you're right about, but hearing that you're right makes the whole situation worse somehow. Like, once you hear that you've been lied to, you start to think that everything is a lie…I know it sounds dramatic, but that's the feeling that I couldn't shake for a while."

Nodding, I sigh. "Yeah, I totally understand what you're saying. You think for years that hearing the truth will make you feel better, but instead it makes you feel betrayed. For so many reasons."

"Yes! Exactly!"

The weight seems to be lifting from Leah with the realization that she's not alone. For me, however, it feels like the weights just keep adding on.

"Well, fast forward, like, thirteen years. My mom writes a post on social media and he comments on it after I do. He reaches out to me on a private message and we start talking. He confesses how he never stopped seeing me as his daughter. His mother still thinks of me as her granddaughter and she is dying to talk to me, so I gave him my phone number. For whatever reason, the fear of him dissipated almost immediately. It didn't help that I had just moved to a new state, after my uncle…"

Sucking in cold air, I purse my lips together.

I see exactly where this is going…

"I was living with family that I barely knew, and I was desperate for a parental figure that I could rely on…so, I thought he was going to be it. We talked every day, all day. It became a bit obsessive but not on my end like most imagined. He was the one who would get upset if I didn't call him after classes or would go out with friends, and he didn't know where I was and when I got home. He even insisted on leaving the video chat open while we slept."

Leah must have seen the obnoxious look on my face because she quickly tried to explain.

"I know, okay. I know it sounds crazy now. Hindsight and all, but at the time, I thought he was just being protective, and I had always wanted a protective father figure in my life. I thought, maybe he's trying to make up for lost time, and maybe it's not as weird as it sounded. My family found out about all the 'attention' I was getting from him and were quick to tell me how inappropriate it was. Again, the signs were all there. I was just seeing what I *wanted* to see, not what was really happening."

"This is bad," I say. "It's going to end badly, isn't it?"

She sighs and pulls at the string on her sleeve again.

"I ended up going home and visiting him. My mom was going through a really hard time then and I wanted to be there for her, but I was also so mad at her. That's a whole other story, but the sun is already starting to set and we don't have time for that one. Just know that she and I were not on good terms at all during that visit."

I nod.

"Well, because of that, he and I spent a lot more time together than I had expected to. He was staying at a friend's house, and I had borrowed my mom's car one night to visit. While he and I were watching a movie on the couch, he put a pillow on his lap and asked me to lay down. Again, thinking like a child, I did. A little girl laying her head on her father's lap is normal, right? I didn't know. That's when he started rubbing my back and my butt. I froze, just like when my uncle had touched me. I didn't know what to do. I left shortly after and he knew he had crossed a line. He didn't say anything, but I knew by his actions."

"Oh, my God."

"I drove home in a panic. Part of me couldn't believe this was happening again, but then the other part of me was worried that I was going to lose the only fatherly connection I had, again. That night I was going to tell my mom what happened, but she wouldn't even talk to me because of all that had happened on that trip already, so I stayed awake on the couch all night trying to figure it all out.

Our relationship was never the same after that. It quickly progressed from father-daughter to romantic. He had told me that once my family found out what had happened, they would never look at me the same…how right he was about that. I hadn't said no, once again, and I didn't want to lose him as a father. I know that sounds so weird, but while he was talking to me like a…"

She pauses to gulp down the guilt and shame.

"A boyfriend…he would still say that he wanted to walk me down the aisle if it didn't work out between us. There was still a glimmer of hope for me that we could get it turned back toward what I really wanted, which was a father."

My mouth is dry and I have no words.

"I wasn't totally blameless though. I lied and played along. He would constantly remind me that my family would hate me for it, and that they would never talk to me again. He told me that no man would ever love me because of what happened, so I—" she stops, tears rolling down her face. "I believed him. God, I know I sound so terrible. I know that I messed up and should have told someone, something…but I couldn't. I knew that the second anyone found out, I would be kicked to the curb and have nothing."

This time I place my hand around Leah. She's crying uncontrollably now. The words are just pouring out of her mouth like vomit.

"I lied to everyone: my therapist, my family I was staying with, and myself. He booked a ticket to come see me in the next state over. I told him that I wasn't sure it was a good idea, and he threatened me with the one thing he knew I didn't want to lose…him. He told me that if I didn't show up he would never talk to me again and any relationship we could have in the future would be demolished. That meant, the sliver of hope of going back was gone. So, like a good little girl, I did what he asked. He paid for everything and I followed the directions."

Leah takes a few deep breaths trying to steady herself.

"What happened when you picked him up?" I ask.

"He had sex with me…"

"He raped you?" I blurt out.

She shakes her head. "No…that's the thing. I can't call it rape because I went there knowing that it was going to happen. I knew that once I lied to everyone around me, it was too late. I had crossed a line that I couldn't turn back from and again…I didn't say no. Did I want it? Of course not, but I was so blinded by the fact that if it came out I would have nobody…that I…I went. That was the worst mistake I could ever have made…"

"You're blaming yourself?" I ask in shock.

"I'm taking responsibility," she shoots back. "I know what I did was wrong. I know that my desire for a father was greater than my ability to think this all through. The signs were there, but I chose to ignore them in hopes that it was all going to be okay. I know that my desire for a father and lies hurt the people around me."

I shake my head. "But that doesn't mean that he should have taken advantage of you. He knew your want for a father. He knew about your uncle, and yet…he took advantage of a vulnerable, broken girl."

Through huge tears, Leah chuckles sadly. "It depends on who you ask."

Wrinkling my forehead, I ask, "What does that mean?"

"Once I was home from the 'visit,' I tried to cut ties. I still was lying to my family because I was scared, but I knew that it had gone too far. It was all out in the open not too long after that and my family was hurt, of course. I lied to them and without context, it looks like I did a heinous thing. After the dust settled and I got to explain my side, they were there for me. They were supportive and understanding. They even went to battle for me against him and anyone who tried to say something nasty about me. What I hadn't realized and what took me way longer than it should have to see, was that they were my parental figures. They were the ones who had my back and loved me unconditionally through it all. Even with the fault that I had in the situation."

She sniffs the tears back and with a quivering lip, she continues.

"It was my mom mainly, who couldn't see past it all. She was hurt and I totally understand that. She thought I had done this purposely to hurt her, though, and that was something I couldn't understand. I love my mom, I love her so much, and I would never do anything to purposely hurt her like that. I'm not that kind of person and for her to think of me like that devastated me. Worse, she told people that version of the story. Her friends, family, my father…They all think of me like a whore," she throws her head back. "God, maybe they're right. Maybe I am a whore. I knew what was going to happen. I was scared, but I should have stayed home. I should have changed my number and gotten rid of all my social medias. I should have told her that night when he first touched me."

Her voice is barely understandable from the amount of tears that are pouring from her eyes. I rub her back lightly and cry with her. This story is hard to digest. I can't imagine how hard it was to live through.

"They're not right, Leah. No matter how you look at it, you were taken advantage of. Do you play a part in it? Yes, you do, but you're able to admit that. No one would blame a mentally unstable person for their actions when they weren't right in the head. How many times do people plead insanity after killing someone and instead of jail time, they are sent to get help? This isn't much different. You were in a vulnerable state. You were broken and bruised from abuse for years before this. He knew that, treated you like a daughter, and then pulled the rug out from under you. *He* was the adult and should have kept it strictly parental. No, I refuse to let you take the blame for this any longer."

I'm surprised by my outburst, and from the look on Leah's face, she is too. The air is cold and a slight breeze picks up. Even with Roxie's sweats on, a chill runs through my body. Taking my arm from her back, I hug myself and cross my arms over my chest. My eyes are having a hard time staying open now.

The day is catching up to me. Taking one hand from across my body, I rub my forehead. A migraine is starting, I can feel it, but I'm not quite sure why.

From the stress, no doubt. Today has been one of the most stressful days I've had in a long time. I still don't have answers, just more questions.

As the throbbing in my head grows, I look from the leaf-covered ground to the empty bench beside me. My eyes feel swollen and I feel as if I can't cry anymore if I tried, yet a single tear escapes my lashes and rolls slowly down my cheek.

For a moment, I just sit. The weight of today, meeting and learning about these people and their sudden absence, is heavy. I can feel it like a pressure coming down on a tiny insect. With my arms still crossed over my chest, I close my eyes and lean my head back. Filling my lungs with air, I hold that position and try to sort through all the madness. If I had known stepping off the bus would have landed me here, I would never have gotten off it in the first place, but here I am, and here I'll stay until I get my feet moving again. With all the energy left inside of me, I stand up on my aching legs.

I have so much more to say to Leah... She left way too soon.

As I mindlessly let my feet guide me to an unknown location, I reflect on the conversation.

Did she even hear what I told her? Why me? Why are they all telling me their stories?

The question is what lingers in my brain for the remainder of my time in Central Park.

Why on Earth, are people opening up to me *of all people?*

As this question rolls around in my head, I notice a large shadow out of the corner of my eye. It grows as it gets closer behind me. A chill runs down my spine and the hair on the back of my neck stands up as I feel the coolness of someone's breath brush the exposed skin under my hairline.

-Chapter Twenty-

"No!" I scream. "Please, God, help!"

My throat is hoarse. My body is aching from all the running. My mind is tired from the stress of these stories. It's hard to find the will to go on, but this person is right there. They are right behind me and whoever it is isn't leaving me alone. The black figure creeping up behind me is now hot on my heels and I'm losing speed.

Trees pass as I run through Central Park praying for a way out. People stand by with no notice of the stressful situation I find myself in. Flight-or-fight mode is starting to wear thin as my aching muscles push toward the end of the park. As I speed up slightly to cross oncoming traffic, I see my father ascend the steps of a beautiful church. The sun is setting behind some buildings, casting an orange hue around us.

A car honks loudly at what I assume is the hooded figure crossing the street behind me.

"Dad!" I scream. "He's coming for me. Please, Dad, help me!"

He's right in front of me yet he's still not listening. The weight of the day takes me down, and my knees buckle sending me to the ground halfway up the steps to the church. The tears are hot as they roll out of my raw, burning eyes and down my cold cheeks. My nose is red from the freezing air and stings as I use the back of the sweater sleeve to wipe it.

"God…" Is all I can say through my sobs.

With my head down, my shoulders crumble with despair. Two shiny black dress shoes appear in my vision. The blinding rays of the sunset burns my eyes, so I squint and use my shaking hand to shield them. My father is looming over me, looking at me, not through me, for the first time today.

Slowly, I get up, my legs shaking both from nerves and weakness. There's a small glimmer of light reflecting off a single tear sliding down his face. It leaves a vulnerable wet trail behind it. Words fail me now that I finally have his attention.

Say something before he leaves you again. I beg myself. *Anything, just don't let him leave you!*

My lips part slightly. "Dad…it's me. It's Savannah. Please—" I sob sucking in a shaky breath. "Please don't run away from me anymore."

His voice is deep and unexpected. His words send a chill down my spine.

"Forgive me, Savannah."

I blink several times in disbelief, my mouth hanging open slightly.

"Forgive me, I don't know what I'm doing."

A flood of tears gush out of my eyes. The gate is open and there's no stopping it.

"What does that mean, Dad? Please, talk to me. Give me something to understand."

He just stands in front of me, still like a stone: unmoving and emotionless.

I throw my head back in frustration and try to calm my hyperventilating body.

"God, please, just talk to me! What is happening here? Why do you keep running from me as if you don't love me? Why are all these girls talking to me about their lives? I need answers, Dad. I feel like I'm losing my mind!"

My voice is harsher than I mean it to be. The built up frustration from the day is finally spilling out and I don't know how to stop it. Looking at him again, his face is softened, but he's still frozen in time, not even blinking.

Then, suddenly without warning, he turns and ascends up the stairs again. I watch in horror as he climbs quickly, opens the door to the church and disappears inside. My sobbing turns into full on blubbering and I collapse in a heap on the stairs. A shadow grows from a figure behind me and I know in my soul it's the person from before.

Crying into my arms as I'm perched on a step, I wait for them to take me. The will to fight and survive is gone and I'm ready for whatever is to come. My body tenses as I feel fingers on my shoulder, but I don't try to get away. I don't budge an inch.

To my surprise, the touch is gentle, not threatening. As I continue to sob, the hand gently pulls for me to turn toward them. I feel their body sitting next to mine on the hard concrete. Tears still in my eyes and curiosity in my mind, I go against my better judgment and turn to face them.

My mind screams as I see the face of the hooded person who had been chasing me. Eyes bulging and mouth dropped, I stare into hazel green eyes with slight wrinkles around them. The black hood is now down, placed gently around the back of the neck. Shoulder length blonde hair is visible. Tears are in her eyes, and mine have stopped at the sight of her.

"You're—you're…" The words are trapped in my throat.

"You?" she laughs. "Yeah, just a bit older."

Blinking several times, I try to understand what's happening. She's wearing a pair of black jeans with the knees cut open. Her trench coat is long with a hood and she has black and pink Vans on to her feet.

Aside from the creepy trench coat, I'd consider wearing that outfit.

"How—how? Why? I—I don't—"

She smiles slightly out of one corner of her mouth, a smile I recognize well.

"It's hard to explain, really. There isn't much I'm allowed to tell you."

"Allowed?" I ask…myself.

She sighs and narrows her eyes slightly with her lips pursed.

"Wait," I say. "Why were you chasing me?"

"You kept running."

My brows furrow as I squint in confusion.

"Sometimes…" she takes a deep breath. " Sometimes we think people in our past are holding us back. We assume that it's their voices controlling the negative thoughts that are in our heads. But, in all reality, it's ourselves. We repeat the words that have been told to us, yes, but it's no longer on the shoulders of those who first stated it. It's now on us."

"What?" I ask, my forehead wrinkled.

"You don't understand now, but you will."

I close my eyes in frustration and take a deep breath.

"Can you please, stop talking in riddles and tell me what is happening?"

"We don't have much time left, but I know you are confused." She folds her hands on her lap and sits up straighter. "What are you looking for?"

I take a moment to think, but I'm exhausted and my mind is fogging up.

"Well, my…our…father. See, he was on the bus and just—"

As I attempt to fill in the events from the day, she stops me.

"It's deeper than that, Savannah. Think."

Shrugging, I say, "I don't know. All I want is peace, really. I'm so tired…"

A sad smile crosses her lips.

"Peace is a condition of inward harmony, Savannah. If you are hurt, offended, or wronged the ability to forgive is inside you. Forget those things which are behind you and move forward."

This hits me hard and tears roll down my face again.

"What if I'm not there yet? I'm not ready to forgive. Those people, they've really hurt me. Some continue to hurt me no matter how much time has passed."

She places a warm, gentle hand on my cheek.

"You need to get there. Holding onto it is delaying your blessings, peace, and mental stability."

The feel of her touch calms my shaking body.

"How?" I whisper. "I've been through so much."

She purses her lips together again, removing her hand from it's comforting spot on my face.

"I'm not saying it's going to be easy, love. I'm saying it's necessary for you to move forward. You're weighing yourself down from holding onto a lifetime of pain. Those chains aren't going to unlock themselves and trust me, you don't want to wake up one day, forty years old still resenting people who hurt you twenty years prior. That's a scary reality that many face."

"How did you do it?" I ask.

She chuckles softly. "Well, my dear, that all depends on you."

I frown my eyebrows at her.

"If you chose to let go and find forgiveness, peace and love, then we will be a joyful individual. If you choose to cling to the pain of your past and present, life will go on without us, and we will end up miserable and alone in the future."

Her words remind me of a saying, but I can't recall who told it me.

"When you smile, the whole world smiles with you…" I say

"When you cry, you cry alone," she finishes.

We smile at each other through the tears. She pats my hands that are sitting in my lap, before reaching into her hooded coat. She pulls out a small, folded piece of paper and slides it into my sweater pocket. As I reach in to take it out, she places her hand on my arm gently.

Shaking her head, she says. "Not yet."

"Why?" I ask.

She smiles sweetly before standing to her feet and descending the church steps. I watch as she carefully takes each step toward the sidewalk.

"Wait!" I plead.

Just like my father had all day, she doesn't turn toward my call. I hang my head in despair again, holding the small paper in my hand as tears drip from my lashes.

Not yet. Is she crazy? If she was really

me, she would know that waiting is not *my strong suit.*

As I begin to unfold the paper, I hear a familiar voice.

"He went in there," Derrota says.

I glance up and see him standing higher up on the landing. Lamentar, close behind him, leans on the building with legs crossed and a playful grin on his face.

-*Chapter Twenty-One*-

Rolling my eyes, I try to find all the strength I have to push myself up. Slipping the folded piece of paper into the back pocket of my jeans, I begin to walk up the stairs. Without realizing, I have changed yet again.

"What could you two possibly be doing here?" I ask.

"Awe, don't be like that! We know you missed us," Lamentar says.

He uncrosses his long legs and begins to walk toward Derrota. Tripping over air, he stumbles forward grabbing his brother for balance. I stifle a laugh as Derrota pushes him off and straightens his clothes.

These two are really something else.

"Anyway," Derrota hisses. "He went inside."

I nod. "Yeah, I saw him go in there."

"Well, are you going to follow him?" Lamentar asks.

Thinking for a moment, I look up at the beautiful church. Something is pulling me toward it, but I want to dismiss it as an urge to follow my father.

"I'm not sure," I state. "I don't really see a point, do you?"

Derrota gives his brother a side eye as Lamentar leans his arm on Derrota's shoulder.

"I don't understand," Derrota says. "You've been running around all day trying to find him, and you're just going to give up right when you have him cornered?"

Biting the inside of my lip, I contemplate this.

"This morning I would have given anything to find him and talk to him about what's going on. There are so many questions still left unanswered, but now…I don't know. It's just different somehow."

"What changed?" Lamentar asks.

Derrota slides his brother's arm off his shoulder, sending him to stumble slightly.

Hesitating, I say, "I—I think I did."

Both of them look at me with furrowed brows. They give me a once over and Lamentar widens his eyes.

"You definitely don't look as put together as you did this morning. Grunge much?"

The brothers look at each other and laugh.

"I'm sorry, did I ask for the fashion police to show up and ruin my day?"

"No, honey, but you should have called 911 because this outfit is screaming for help."

Derrota pretends to hide his laughter, but clearly wants me to see he agrees with his brother.

"Once again, you guys are useless!" I yell.

Crossing my arms, I look out at the last

of the sun setting behind the building. It's beginning to get dark and I'm not sure what to do now. Going back would take me God knows how long, and all paths *did* lead me here…

After the chuckle twins finish their hyena laughter, they both put one hand on either shoulder. The weight of their unexpected arms makes me slump a bit.

"Listen," they say at the same time.

"If you want to turn around right now and never look back, we would understand," Derrota says.

"It's not like you're really cut out for this anyway," Lamentar finishes.

I narrow my eyes at them. "Not cut out?" I seethe.

"Not everyone is able to handle the truth. It's nothing to be ashamed of," Lamentar states.

"You should probably just give up now, don't you think? I mean, your hesitation says it all, Savannah. You're not ready." Derrota squeeze my shoulder slightly.

Shrugging them off, I say, "You two are pathetic. Excuse me."

Pushing past them, I stomp up the church stairs.

"Are you sure you want to do this?" I hear one of them call. "He's only going to break your heart again."

Stopping, I thinking about those words. Taking a deep breath, I swirl around to face them.

"He can only break my heart if I have expectations. Even if I don't get answers from my father—I have to try. If it fails then…then I move on. That's the only option left."

Tears sting my eyes and make my nose tingle. I turn back and push myself toward the beautifully, hand carved door.

Please, I pray. *Please let me find* something *in here that will help me find answers.*

For a moment I stand at the door twiddling my fingers and contemplating. This move is scary for reasons I don't quite understand, but I *know* that once I open this door, life will never be the same. The traffic behind me begins to muffle and my eyes focus on the metal handle on the door.

The air around me is cool, but a slight perspiration builds above my brow and my palms are clammy. I reach out two shaky hands and slowly open the double doors with tense muscles.

Immediately, my eyes encounter darkness, and I blink several times to get them to adjust. Squinting, I see rows of candles against the wall. Some are lit but most aren't. A woman kneels with a long, slim stick in her hand. Her thick, curly black hair brings my attention to focus. Again, I blink several times, not sure if I'm truly seeing her.

"Aunt Angela?" I ask, close to a whisper.

She lights the stick from one candle, brings the flaming wood to another one and lights the wick. Looking over her shoulder at me she smiles slightly.

"Come light your candle, hon," she says.

-Chapter Twenty-Two-

Slowly, I walk over to her, afraid if I move too quickly she'll fade away. My knees crack as I kneel next to her and take the stick from her slender fingers. I can feel the heat from the fire coming toward my body, so I quickly light a candle and blow out the flame.

Looking over, I see that her head is bowed. I follow suit, not really sure what I'm praying for. Being close to her makes me feel like I'm home. Like I never want to leave her side or run off again.

She doesn't even seem worried.

After what feels like an eternity, my aunt

rises to her feet and walks further into the church. I follow with little expectation as to what we will find. The sanctuary is beautiful. The floor to ceiling windows on either side are covered in the most glorious stained glass I have ever seen. Ahead is a towering crucifix with tremendous detailing on both the wooden cross and Jesus himself.

Seeing him hanging so lifelike on the wooden beams makes my heart ache, yet gives me clarity simultaneously. My aunt sits in one of the pews in the back and I slide in next to her. She looks sad, yet stoic.

"I'm so sorry," I whisper. "I can explain why I left you—"

"Shhh," she pats my knee. "It's okay. You had to find your way. I knew that you would find your way back when you were ready."

I squeeze her soft hand and smile. Once again tears build up in my eyes but I try desperately to hold them back. She smiles softly back at me before bowing her head. As a tear escapes, I look back to the altar at the front of the church. To my surprise, I recognize all the young ladies kneeling before the giant statue. My eyes widen when Joy comes up next to me with her hand reached out.

"Oh my gosh, Joy!" I almost screech. "You're okay!"

Leaping out of my seat, I throw my arms around her tiny body and hug her tight. After releasing her, I look into her sad eyes. She gives me a bright smile, taking my hand and attempts to guide me toward the front. I hesitate, looking back at my aunt.

What if she disappears on me too?

With her head still bowed, she looks up enough just to meet my eyes. The smile on her face tells me it's okay to proceed as if she read my mind.

"I'm not going anywhere," she whispers reassuringly.

Taking a deep breath, I allow Joy to lead the way to the front of the church. We pass by mostly empty pews, until we come across a woman and what looks to be her mother. The young lady has dark brown hair pulled back into a ponytail and square glasses like the ones I usually wear at home. Her round face feels familiar, but not like the other faces I've seen today.

She seems to be a few years older than I am and as our eyes lock, a feeling of calm rushes over me. Her lips curl into a faint smile that doesn't show her teeth and somewhere deep down, I feel my soul pulling toward her like families do. Somehow I know, she is supposed to be in my life. Her mother is just as beautiful as the woman, with the same features, yet older. As we pass by them, I feel the urge to turn back and hug them both.

I hear the woman say, "You should thank the blessed motha that you're here"

Her Bronx accent is strong and it brings a smile to my face. There's no doubt I'm going to meet them again. Maybe in another life. There is an unspoken connection that I know in my heart God placed between us.

Drawing near to the podium, I see all the girls from my day lined up and kneeling with their hands folded. Joy lets go of my hand, joining them at the end of the line. There's a gap between Mary and Leah, where I assume I'm supposed to kneel, but my body is frozen. Tears build up in my eyes yet again, for reasons I don't understand.

Mary grabs my hand and gives it a slight squeeze. I look down at her as she smiles up at me.

"He's been waiting for you," she says softly.

My watery eyes widen. "You've seen Dad?"

I kneel next to her with curiosity and confusion flooding my brain.

"Not your dad. Our Father," Leah whispers.

My head swivels on my neck to face her. She looks okay, not great, but okay enough to smile. More than she could telling me her horrible story. Then it all floods back to my mind. Their stories all seem to collide with my brain, clearing it in a weird way. I take a deep breath through my nose, closing my eyes. Exhaling through my mouth, I feel a strange warmth rush through my veins.

Eyes still closed, as if in an out- of-body experience, I see myself from high above. The girls have gone, leaving me alone at the altar, yet I sense a powerful presence. For a moment, I'm fearful. Chills run over me sending goosebumps across my skin. The air is still.

"My beloved," I hear. *"Stop searching for something to fill the void in your heart and allow me to heal you."*

Snapping back to reality, my eyes shoot open. Tears stream down my cheeks. My eyes are on the cross in front of me and the whole room melts away. Pure white engulfs me. The altar and I are the only things in the room, yet I don't feel alone.

"Savannah," I hear audibly.

The voice is powerful, yet gentle. Loud, yet soft. Booming, yet quiet.

"Jesus," is all I can bring myself to say.

"Beloved, I will never leave you nor forsake you. Before you were in your mother's womb, I knew you. Your hairs are numbered and I know the plans I have for you."

Large drops of tears roll down my face.

"But you *did* leave me!" I shout in sobs. "You allowed all those terrible things to happen to me!"

"Oh, my child." There's pain in His voice. "Don't you understand? I have cried when you cried. I have hurt when you hurt. All those tears I caught in the palm of my hand and I *promise* to take the bad intended for you and make it good."

I hear Him sniff back tears.

"All you have to do is trust me."

"Father," I whisper. "What about the things *I've* done…how can you love me when even my own parents can't?"

"I have loved you with a love you can't understand. Even in your darkest times, I was there with you. I carried you through the fire, waiting for you to turn to me. There is nothing you could do, no place you can hide, that I won't rescue you."

A bright light glows high above me. It's intense, so I use my right arm to shield it from my eyes.

"Take my hand, Beloved. Have faith. Abide in me and I shall abide in you. That is my promise and my word never returns void."

"What about the others?" I ask. "Father, they need you too!"

"My beautiful child." I hear a smile in His voice. "You are weary and weak. Come to me and I shall restore your soul."

As I reach my hand out to Him, I hear someone yelling my name faintly.

"I'm here!" I yell.

"Child—"

"Savannah…"

"God! Don't leave me," I cry. "Please, God, don't leave me!"

"Abide in me…" His voice is faint.

"Savannah…"

The voice is growing in strength.

"No!" I scream.

"Savannah…Savannah!"

-*Chapter Twenty-Three*-

My eyes shoot open.

I see a white, popcorn ceiling. A blinding light shines down on me from the fan whooshing above. I blink several times, taking in the environment. There's a slight aroma of lavender in the air. My head is being held up by a stiff pillow, while my legs are parallel to my body. I feel my hands folded over my stomach and I'm afraid to move.

"Savannah?" A familiar voice speaks.

Slowly I move my head to the right and I see a middle aged woman sitting on a puffy black office chair. The high back looms over her. She has dark brown hair with hints of grey streaks. Her bangs hang over the rim of her glasses and her dark eyes are wide.

"Are you okay?" she asks.

Concern is written all over her face.

I push myself up with my elbows and look at her. Reality is starting to set in, causing my memory to defog. Nodding, I sit up straighter and place my feet on the floor.

Clearing my throat, I ask, "What happened?"

My therapist leans back in her chair and sighs in relief. She pats her forehead with a cloth of some kind.

"You were in a hypnotic state. Unfortunately, you were under for longer than I had expected." She pats the back of her neck. "I was about to call an ambulance because you weren't responding to the usual methods to bring your mind back."

As she speaks, I look around her holistic room. The tapestries hanging from the wall are beautiful and abstract. A book case sits in the corner filled with books of all shapes and sizes.

She has a hippie look to her that I didn't notice before. On the desk next to her is a necklace with a thin chain and large, round pendant.

"Was I really hypnotized?" I ask, skeptically.

She nods, holding her dark hair back into a pony tail.

"Yeah, you were. Do you recall anything?"

Thinking for a moment, I remember everything about the journey in New York City. The girls, the stories, the fear.

"I don't understand it all, but yes, I remember it."

She leans on her knees waiting for me to explain my journey.

"Don't we have to go? Like, isn't our time up?"

My therapist narrows her eyes in confusion and says, "We booked a two hour session today, remember? I wanted to give you all the time you needed for this."

Slowly, I nod, biting the inside of my lip. I try to break down the intense dream as quickly as I can, but my head is still spinning from it all.

"I think…" Pausing, I let my brain sort out the chaos. "I think the girls who helped me through the city…I think they were me."

Clearing her throat, she asks, "What makes you say that?"

I rub my forehead. "All their stories were mine. Their clothes were mine. Their mannerisms. In one way or another, they were all me."

Again, she nods silently.

The air conditioning kicks on, sending a chill down my spine. I hug my knees close to my body and tug on my black sweater sleeves. At this point, I know I should have tears rolling down my face, but it's as if my body can't make anymore.

Had I cried while I was hypnotized?

The crusty feeling on my lashes indicates that I had.

"What do you think that means?" I ask.

"Well, Savannah, it could mean that you're processing your pain in different ways.

Compartmentalizing if you will. It could mean that when it comes to your hurt, you're hiding it away in spots you don't allow yourself to think of or go near. Some of these things, you've never even brought up in our sessions."

A tear rolls down, but I know that more are hiding inside of me.

"I don't want to dwell on that life anymore."

"So, what are you going to do?" she asks.

Looking at her, I furrow my brows and frown.

"Before we placed you under I explained that one of two things would happen when you woke. You will either learn from what you saw, let go and move forward, or you'll lose yourself deeper in the sadness and frustration."

Contemplating this, I bit the inside of my lip. My heart is racing as my mind replays scene after scene. Mary, Leah, Purdy, Vanity, all their faces flash in my head. Joy's face is last to pop up and tears rush to my eyes. A faint taste of lead fills my mouth.

That little girl doesn't deserve to live a life of constant negativity. I think silently as the tears slowly roll down my face. *That little girl has been through enough and if I could tell her one more thing, I'd say to…*

"Just keep going…" I whisper.

She breathes a sigh. "Is this a breakthrough I hear?"

I smile slightly. "God is good, right?"

She nods.

"He brought me out of that life and placed me in a family that loves me."

The gate is open. Tears flow effortlessly down my face and drip from my chin onto my knees.

"It would be a disservice to them…and myself if I allowed that life to keep creeping in, right?"

Again, she nods, smiling slightly. "The thing is, Savannah. Your past will always try to creep in. It's up to you not to let it affect your life. An addict will always be an addict and has to work daily on staying away from that life. Trauma works the same way. The fear will make its way to your brain, but you have the power to stop it from making its way to your heart."

I sniff and wipe my nose with the back of my sweater allowing her words to marinate in my brain.

"It seems to me that there are two paths being laid out in front of you here, Savannah. There's the path that leads back down to hurt and pain that keeps happening over and over in a vicious cycle, and there's a path of resistance. The path less traveled if you will. That is where you will find that when God closes a door, somewhere he opens a window."

Ah, The Sound of Music. I think. *Where's Julie Andrews when you need her to sing her way into your life?*

Sucking in a deep breath, I wipe the stream of tears away. My therapist looks at the small tree carved into a clock on her desk and snaps her tongue.

"Keep thinking and we'll talk more tomorrow about your next move, okay?"

Her smile is bright and relaxed now. I

nod and smile weakly back at her. She pats my knee before standing and leading me toward the door. As I emerge from the room, I see my Aunt Angela and Uncle Derek sitting on the leather, coffee colored couch in the waiting room. There's a noise machine humming faintly in the corner.

As they see me, smiles spread across their faces. My aunt places her magazine on the coffee table, before moving her puffy black hair off her shoulder to pull her purse in place. My uncle runs a hand through his full grey hair before standing. I run over and throw my arms around her waist, embracing her tightly.

"It's okay," she whispers. "I'm not going anywhere."

I feel her tears splash on my shoulder before letting go.

"What am I, wood?" my uncle jokes.

He pretends to flick me and I smile brighter giving him a big hug as well.

"Should we stop for some apps before heading home?" my aunt asks.

I nod wiping my eyes.

"I definitely need a drink," I say.

My therapist stands in the doorway of her office, leaning against the post and smiles with tears. She, of all people, knows what this moment means to me. As we exit the office, I reach into my back jean pocket to get my phone and a folded piece of paper falls to the floor. I frown in confusion as I bend to pick it up.

After unfolding it, I see a page from my college Spanish vocabulary notes staring back at me.

Derrota: noun – Defeat

Lamentar: verb – Regret

My eyes widen at the definitions and my hands begin to shake. Recalling the moment on the steps with my older self, I slowly flip the paper over. I gasp, my breath getting caught in my throat. Larger tears fill my eyes as I read, in my handwriting, a note I don't recall writing.

-*Chapter Twenty-Four*-

The smell of fresh brewed coffee assaults my nose as I drag my aging body downstairs. No matter how many times I make my way through the large, five bedroom house, it still captures me with awe. Beneath me is lush carpeting that feels soft on my aching feet. Cautiously I step, allowing myself to relish in the silence for a few seconds longer.

"Nothing is more important than the moment you're in."

I recall this saying from a faint memory or a dream.

A tall, broad man stands at the stove with his back facing me. I smile knowing that he is in his element in the kitchen and that he doesn't even know I'm closing in on him. The sound of hissing bacon grows as I tip-toe my way across the hardwood floor. Just as I'm about to wrap my arms around him sweetly, two little kids screech and attack me with hugs around my legs from behind the counter.

"Mommy!" They yell in unison.

Swirling around, my husband grabs at his heart and closes his eyes. I crouch down and wrap my arms tightly around the little toddlers.

"Never sneak up on a man with a spatula," he says. "That's kitchen etiquette 101."

He smiles brightly and starts chasing the three of us with his spatula in the air. The kids screech again with laughter, and we run quickly to the living room before being trapped between the big, navy couch and the crazed chef. My husband grabs our son and pretends to pat his bottom with the kitchen tool, while tickling his side with his other hand. I turn on our daughter, throw her on the couch and tickle her stomach.

The house fills with laughter.

The bacon summons my husband back to the stove with a slight pop. Standing, he smiles at me and rushes to attend to the food. The couch is soft and I allow it to engulf my body as I sink further into it. Closing my eyes, I say a silent prayer of gratitude from this seemingly perfect life that I find myself in.

"Ugh," I groan.

My daughter's sweet face is inches from mine after plopping down hard on top of my stomach. Her red hair curtains her wide blue eyes. Soft freckles scatter across her pure white skin and wrinkled nose.

"Mommy, your breath stinks," she says.

"Just wait until I have coffee," I mutter out of the side of my mouth.

"Me too!" My son chimes in.

He runs over and smashes his body right into my legs before attempting to climb up on me. His sandy blonde hair matches my artificially colored hair almost to a tee. The Irish twins stare up at me lovingly, melt my heart. I kiss their soft little cheeks before sliding them onto the couch. My bones crack a little as I rise to my feet. A long haired cat with colors similar to my daughter's, purrs through my legs.

"Good morning, Barry," I say.

Making my way back to the kitchen, I see my husband spooning eggs onto four different plates, leaving just a little taste for our fur-baby's bowl. Sitting on top of the island counter, I see an already made cup of coffee with steam gently rising from the rim. Smiling, I wrap my arms around his midsection and lay my head on his back.

"What did I do to get so lucky?" I ask.

He laughs. "What did I do this time, buns?"

Turning around on his heels, he kisses my forehead before I let him go.

"You're just being you."

He smiles brightly. "You're crazy."

I sneak a nibble of bacon off one of

the plates before grabbing my hot cup of coffee and taking a big whiff of the hazelnut scent. Glancing at my calendar, I see the day's events laid out neatly. The color coded words brighten up the white paper on the silver fridge.

Tuesday:

Morning meeting – 9am

Client meeting – Noon

Kids soccer practice – 4:30 pm

Therapy appointment – 6pm

Blowing on my coffee and studying the words, I take a sip. The roof of my mouth screams from the heat and I wince. The clock on the stove reads eight forty-five which means I have about three seconds until my…

The video device on my island counter begins to ring and I smile knowingly. I touch my husband's back gently as I pass him to answer the call. The kids continue to run around chasing each other as I press the flashing green button. My best friend and business partner's face pops up. Her dark brown hair is pulled up as usual and her square glasses reflect her side of the video call. Our similar round faces sit next to each other on a split screen.

"Morning, Love," I say.

"You're still in your robe?" she asks. "What's wrong? Tell me right now."

I smile brightly at her, take another sip of my coffee and glance around the room. My husband sets the table for us to have breakfast. My kids laugh hysterically at each other for no apparent reason. My daughter bends over and picks up the cat as if he's a toy.

Letting out a soft sigh with a smile still plastered on my face, I say, "Honestly, Elle. Nothing. Nothing at all."

Across the room, I see a framed torn piece of paper sitting on a decorative table behind our couch. The first moment I read it comes flooding back to my memory. I envision a younger, more vulnerable me standing in the middle of a therapist's office, surrounded by the only two people she had in the world. The single torn piece of paper that I still don't remember writing, stares back at me.

I purse my lips together, trying not to cry as the feelings rush back through me. Knowing the contents of that paper by heart, my mind starts reciting the words as if on cue:

Dear Savannah,

I have so much I want to tell you. I want to tell you all that you have coming toward you so you don't make the same mistakes, but in the end, those mistakes are what make us who we are. If you avoid them, you'll avoid some of the best parts of your life. All I'm going to say is be happy with who you are. Never give up on yourself, your loved ones, or God. Never lose your faith because that is all you have to hold onto when life gets rocky and trust me it happens often. Remember who you are deep down, and don't let anyone take that away from you. Don't forget to love. Love everyone you meet, love what you do, love who you are, and love even when love doesn't seem like enough. You will make it through whatever is thrown at you, but not alone. Lean on God, trust not on your own understanding, and life won't be as hurtful as it was intended to be. Lastly, you aren't defined by your past or what's happened to you. You're defined by who you become and what you make of what happened. Don't forget to forgive yourself as well as others. That's just as important in your healing process. Above all, just keep going...Psalm 46:5

Love,

The best version of you

-Word From The Author-

First, thank you. Thank you for picking up this book to read and invest time in. Thank you for choosing my words to entertain you and I pray that it did. There are no words to truly relay the amount of courage it took to place this book in your hands on my part and I hope it meant something to you.

I have been writing since I was six years old. The stories I have made were almost always a reflection of my emotions at the time and I'm thankful that I have that innate way of storytelling inside me. Yet, this story is by far the hardest thing I have ever written. The vulnerability that comes with telling a story so close to your heart is intense. Sharing your story with strangers in hopes that it can help them with their own pain and exposing parts of your life is one of the most difficult things to do. All I can do is pray that it was worth reliving all of this a second time. If only ONE of you was taught something from this story, than it was worth it.

The purpose of this story is to share that everyone has difficulties. Everyone has skeletons in their closets and those skeletons can take a toll on us if we don't let them out. I have carried around the burden of my past for many years and for me, this was a release of that burden. The way to let go is to acknowledge that it happened, not sweep it under the rug. The way to grow from your experiences is to claim it as your past, learn from what happened and take that knowledge forward.

My hope for you is that you will drop the weight of your past and move forward, living a happy and healthy life. My hope is that you see that you are not alone and that you can overcome your issues because so many others have before you. My hope is that you learn that you are a diamond that may be covered in dust, but it doesn't dull your sparkle. Rise from the ashes as I have and show off who you are. Your past doesn't define you. Your past isn't who you are. It was a sentence in the story of your life, NOT a life sentence.

-Acknowledgments-

I honestly have so much to say and so many people to thank. I'm terrified I'm going to leave people out, so if you are left out, please know that I am so thankful for you and your role in my life. I'm sorry if I've missed you.

First, as always, I have to thank God for His everlasting love in my life! I know without a shadow of a doubt that I would not have made it this far in my life without His grace, love, and guidance. I have a beautiful life now and that is purely because He took the bad and turned it into good. Thank you, Jesus, for all you have done, are doing, and will do in my future!

Second, I have to thank my amazing husband, Rob. You're such a light in my world. Your love, support, advice, and help never goes without notice, and I am beyond thankful for you every day! I not only have a best friend in you, but a love like no other. Thank you for loving me and helping me through my past by giving me a future. I couldn't have done it without you.

My two beautiful children. I'm torn if I ever want you to read this, but if you do, know that you are the light that came out of a very dark tunnel. God had many plans in my life and getting through all of this in order to meet your father and have you two was part of that plan. I am a better person because I'm your mom and I thank you for that. Without you, I wouldn't have known the true unconditional love I could give to someone else. I love you with all my heart and soul.

My best friend, business partner, other

half of my soul, and sister, Lauren. No restrictions apply with you! I know in my heart of hearts that the only reason I worked at the bank was to meet you and have an everlasting friendship. I can never thank you enough for always being there for me, loving me when I have nothing left to give, and being there for my family in ways most friends don't bother. YOU are a light in my life that I couldn't live without.

Aunt Angela and Uncle Derek. I'm sure you are tired of hearing it at this point, but THANK YOU. You're love and devotion to me for all these years is something I'm still working on believing that I deserve. You have loved me in my lowest lows, when I couldn't love you back, and when I pushed you away. While writing this story, the symbolism of your constant presence in my life was so great because it really happened. I could not be the person I am today without you two, and for that I will be forever grateful!

My Antipasta and Uncle Mike. Over the years, distance has caused us to lose constant contact, but never have you left my hearts. I know that I wouldn't have made it through my early years without your love and guidance. I also know, I wouldn't have the faith in God and love for Him if I didn't have you to teach me early on.

To some notable family members who were there for me throughout my years: Gram, Aunt Donna, Mama Jane, Noni, Poppi, Harold, Filissa, Laura C., Desiree, Grant, Kylee, Matt, David, and Mike. You all mean so much to me and I'm so thankful to have you in my life. Whether you know it or not, you have helped me just by loving me. Thank you for never giving up on me!

To my parents: thank you for the lessons.

To the teachers that helped me, even when you didn't know you were. Debbie Cluff, Stephanie Dukarm, Lisa Cota, and Jimmy Allen. You all have played a role in my life that only someone with a huge heart could do. God made you teachers to touch the lives of so many, mine included. I wish more teachers were like you all. Thank you for all your hard work and love.

Along the same lines, Steve Schulman, Diedrich Wasserbauer, Amy Wasserbauer, Adam Van Liew, and Amy Van Liew. You all hold such a special place in my heart. Three of you started as teachers, yet you and your families became my friends. I can never thank you enough for being there for me when I had nothing and no one. Adam and Amy, your huge hearts and love has not been forgotten. You took me in and gave me a home when I had nothing to give back in exchange. I love you all from the bottom of my heart!

There has been a plethora of friends who have been there for me when I was down. Most of us have lost touch, but that doesn't mean that your time in my life wasn't meaningful. Shawn, Collette, Carlos, Mandy, Sharon, Stephanie, Steve, Randi, Adelaine, Amanda, and Jessie. I love you all and I thank you for your roll in my life. Big or small, you've touched my heart.

My beta readers! Thank you so much for

your feedback and willingness to take time out of your schedule to help me work on this story. Your suggestions and advice did not go unnoticed, and I'm so grateful that you guys volunteered! Thank you so very much!

Before I go, I want to thank YOU. The person reading this book. Thank you for spending the time to read my story. This story is not only mine because I wrote it, but it's mine because I lived it. Thank you for giving me the chance to entertain you and I hope that I did. There are many more stories inside me, so stay tuned! If you would kindly write a review on Amazon and recommend to your friends and family, I would greatly appreciate it. Again, thank you for your trust, love and support!

-About the Author-

Kayla Scutti is a married mother of two. She's the co-owner and CEO of Arbuckle Publishing House, where she helps other authors find their dreams. Helping other people has always been a passion of Kayla's, sometimes to a fault. Kayla has her BFA in Creative Writing for Entertainment and continues to seek out ways to learn and grow personally, spiritually, and with her business. Aside from writing and reading, Kayla loves spending time with her small family. Hiking, camping, watching The Office, Gilmore Girls, and Friends, exploring new places, playing boardgames, and going to church are some of her favorite ways to spend her time.